THE CHAUFFEUR

Also by Howard Norman

The Northern Lights (1987)

The Bird Artist (1994)

The Museum Guard (1998)

The Haunting of L. (2002)

THE CHAUFFEUR

STORIES

Howard Norman

Picador USA   New York

Picador® USA is a registered trademark and is used by St. Martin's Press under license from Pan Books Limited.

www.picadorusa.com

Library of Congress Cataloging-in-Publication Data

Norman, Howard A.
    The chauffeur : stories / Howard Norman.—1st Picador USA ed.
        p.   cm.
    Contents: The chauffeur—Kiss in the Hotel Joseph Conrad—Jenny Aloo—Old swimmers—Laughing and crying—Catching heat—Milk train—Whatever Lola wants.
    ISBN 0-312-28793-3
    I. Title.
PR9199.3.N564 C47 2002
813'.54—dc21

                                                              2001056100

The Chauffeur previously appeared in *Off the Beaten Path: Stories of Place*, published by North Point Press in 1998.

First Picador USA Edition: April 2002

10   9   8   7   6   5   4   3   2   1

For Emma, Estelle, Essie

I thank Ande Zellman for her encourgement; "Old Swimmers" is dedicated to her. "Whatever Lola Wants" is for Charlotte Potok; "Jenny Aloo" is for Stanley Plumly; "Laughing and Crying" is for Richard LeMon.

Contents

Introduction

The Norman Context

By Thomas Mallon

HOWARD NORMAN'S FOUR WORKS OF FICTION AMOUNT
to only about a thousand pages and seem somehow less like
an oeuvre than an eccentric stash, similar to the cryptic paintings and antique radios and wooden bird decoys that line the
pages of the books themselves. And yet, for all their humble
clutter, they prove exquisite, like pieces of folk art whose sim-
plicity postpones a sly impact.

A naturalist and a translator of Native American tales,
Norman came late to his career as a novelist. When he published *The Northern Lights*, in 1987, he was approaching 40,
and even that book—the story of young Noah Krainik in
rural 1950s Manitoba—hesitated, like a boy's changing voice,
unsure whether it wanted to be a collection of set pieces (the

mad quilting woman, the beautiful, nude-bathing Norwegian wife) or a full-throated novel, which it becomes only toward the end, when Noah, having survived the loss of his boyhood friend Pelly Bay, moves to Toronto to help his abandoned mother rejuvenate the movie theater where she worked as a young woman.

If you read *The Northern Lights* after you've read Norman's other books—and thereby made acquaintance with his patterns and preoccupations—you won't be surprised to find that the theater is more important than the movies it shows; or that a Cree Indian family is living in the projectionist's booth; or that the accident that kills young Pelly is beautifully macabre (his unicycle falls through the ice). Norman's heroes, who always tell their own first-person stories, are boys and young men, orphaned or otherwise sundered from their parents. Despite what Pelly's uncle Sam says about how "people should not become their losses," the protagonists are a combination of what they've lost and what they can't have, the latter sure to be an enchanting and impossible young woman.

In Noah's case, that's his cousin Charlotte (herself an orphan), "a very opinionated girl," whose birthmark betokens "a rare, stubborn character." And Charlotte is nothing compared with Imogen Linny, the object of desire in Norman's third novel, *The Museum Guard*, set in Halifax in the late 1930s. This time the hero, DeFoe Russet, has lost his parents in a zeppelin accident. From the age of 9, he's been raised in the Lord Nelson Hotel by his randy uncle Edward, who re-

sembles the life-loving panders of Renaissance comedy, trying, sometimes cruelly, to inject a bit of friskiness into his
solemn nephew. DeFoe guards a gallery in the Glace Museum
not far from the one Edward looks after. Imogen (another
orphan) works at an even quieter job, caretaking the Jewish
cemetery in Halifax. Her romance with DeFoe is marked by
protracted periods of "celibacy and quarrels," her moodiness
and passive aggression leaving the poor young man quite beside himself, especially when he's beside her: "Often I found
I had to circle around her with words. . . . Even lying next to
her in bed, pitch-black room, or a strip of light from her
kitchen floor lamp showing under the closed door, she did
not always seem directly approachable."

Imogen's headaches and scoldings and mixed sexual signals
prefigure the difficulty she will present after developing an
obsessive identification with the subject of a painting, *Jewess
on a Street in Amsterdam*, on loan to the Glace from Nazi-
threatened Holland. "Here's what I think," she tells the sweet,
literal DeFoe. "I think she's living a true life and I am not."
So Imogen decides to live the Jewess's life, to continue the
existence of the artist's wife who modeled for the painting
and was killed by the Germans after Kristallnacht. Imogen's
madness begins with her determination to commune—all
alone, overnight—with the canvas. DeFoe, in one of the wild
gestures that eventually burst forth from Norman's polite heroes, steals it for her.

Norman always tells you the worst in the first paragraph

or even sentence. "The painting I stole for Imogen Linny, *Jewess on a Street in Amsterdam*, arrived to the Glace Museum, here in Halifax, on September 5, 1938": So begins *The Museum Guard*. And so began *The Northern Lights*: "My father brought home a radio. 'It's got a sender and a receiver,' he said. 'Now you can talk to people other than yourselves.' He fit the earphones over my head. And the first news I heard was that my friend Pelly Bay had drowned." The author doesn't just tip his hand; he spreads it faceup on the table and then takes you back to events occurring well before whatever explosion he's already detonated. The effect is peculiarly artful, the disclosures creating the very suspense they ought to be destroying. One wonders, uneasily, during the muffled comedy that usually follows the opening revelations, how the books will break out of their Cornell-boxed charms and get to their announced tragedies. *The Museum Guard*, peopled as it is with lecherous Uncle Edward and the forbearing curator, Mr. Connaught, and the pretentious tour guide, Miss Delbo, reads almost like a Friday-night Britcom—daffy staff in provincial museum—until Uncle Edward gets shot and Imogen takes her delusion to Amsterdam and DeFoe waits for news of her from prison.

By the end, the novel is about art's transformational power and how—as in Norman's books—that power often depends on what's at the margins. In the shop window in the *Jewess* painting, which DeFoe ponders every day from his guard's vantage, are "all sorts of toothbrushes. The toothbrushes made one laugh. They quickly put me in a good mood. But then I looked close up at the Jewess' face; I was sunk from that mood in a second."

In *The Bird Artist* (1994), the novel for which he is best known, Norman made the hero a painter. Fabian Vas, who turns 20 in 1911, lives in Witless Bay, Newfoundland, and is learning to draw and paint birds via a correspondence course. His mother has an affair with the local lighthouse keeper when his father is off hunting; and Fabian, dreading the marriage his parents have arranged for him, is of course smitten with someone difficult—a willful, funny, alcoholic redhead named Margaret Handle:

> "You are a blunt woman, Margaret."
>
> "Fabian, dear, I'm only exactly as blunt as life is, forgive the preachy sentence. You're going to marry a stranger. Your mother is adultering nightly. Your father's got one hell of a homecoming in store. How much more bluntness do you want?"

We know that Fabian's impending nuptials will be the least of his woes, since the book's first paragraph has already had him announcing the real catastrophe. "I am a bird artist, and have more or less made a living at it. Yet I murdered the lighthouse keeper, Botho August, and that is an equal part of how I think of myself." So we wait, thoroughly attentive, for Fabian's id to break through his fastidiousness. (During nervous spells, he drinks coffee; DeFoe Russet irons shirts.)

The Bird Artist's bleak Newfoundland landscape will turn gaudy with blood and recrimination, and at the end, the book's melodrama will be replicated in a supposedly penitential mural that Fabian paints for the local church:

> Botho stands in the topmost window of the lighthouse, black wings spreading from his back, three splotches of blood on his nightshirt. He is the presiding angel of Witless Bay. . . . On the rotted dock at the southernmost point of the harbor, Margaret is a grown woman riding her bicycle.

Most novelists—more troubled than they like to admit by the enduring equation of the picture and the thousand words—seek to achieve a painterly vividness in their work. But Norman seems unsatisfied until, in the course of each book, his heroes can transform their spoken narratives into actual pictures. Once in prison, DeFoe Russet has "a view of Halifax Harbour and can see the topmost masts of the historical schooners. Hour after hour, that is my framed view." Near the end of *The Northern Lights*, when Noah arrives in Toronto, he sleeps in a room with two portraits of himself that were done by the now dead Pelly back in Manitoba.

Any good novel will take you out of your own world; ones

that actually put you into another one—instead of leaving you in the mere suspended state of "reading"—are rare. Norman's are among them. Fictional kingdoms like his are so strongly imagined as to be a bit oppressive, and their writers labor under something of a compulsion to re-create them from book to book. What makes these novelists unique is also what circumscribes them; their greatest strength is necessarily their worst weakness. An extreme example of such repetition can be found in the work of the English novelist Anita Brookner, whose lonely London flat dwellers need to get out more but simply can't and finally shouldn't: too much activity would kill their odd reality.

Norman's novels are all variations on a dream. His tricky northern landscapes, both homey and stark, have a demon's face glowering up through the ice. *The Museum Guard* may play itself out a bit slowly toward the end, but the author's work is generally as lean as a sled's runner. In an age of biblio size-worship—a comically obvious affliction among ambitious male novelists—Norman writes to exactly the right modest length, just as Alice Munro, who also works the Canadian past and may be the greatest contemporary writer of fiction in English, has found a natural habitat not in the novel but in the long short story. As DeFoe tells his uncle Edward at one point in *The Museum Guard*, "What I'm saying is some things are my big subjects. . . . They might be smaller, but they fit my life. So leave me alone about it."

What for another writer would be motifs are, in Norman,

almost the melody. Those radios, for instance: They're not the symbol of long-distance projection and communion; they're the fact. In *The Northern Lights* (a book Norman says he began as a radio play), a shortwave set may bring the news of Pelly's death, but it was another radio, shared by Pelly and Noah, that once took the boys far from Quill, Manitoba:

> It was a brown Grundig-Majestic, about two feet high. . . . At nine o'clock, *Great Books* connected us to the libraries of the world. This program began with the reader, Fabian Bennet, announcing in a British accent, "Here, once again," then a background voice hushing him. Bennet would say, "So sorry," and lower his voice.

At one point in his story, when Noah has an attack of misanthropy, he doesn't drink coffee or iron shirts; he dismantles and reassembles a shortwave set. He has to shake the feeling that Pelly "drowned inside the radio," just as, in a heartbreaking story of Norman's called "Jenny Aloo," an Eskimo woman feels certain her son has disappeared into a jukebox. In *The Museum Guard*, the Fabian Bennet figure is Ovid Lamartine, whose dire broadcasts from Europe in the fall of 1938 help lure both Imogen and Uncle Edward toward calamity. Nothing in fiction succeeds like obsession; Norman's is the airwaves ridden by birds and sound alike.

He may set his books in 1911 and 1938 and 1959, but one can't really call him a historical novelist. The novels aren't heavily textured with period detail, and the author's dialogue, fine at fostering the illusions it's designed to, is more charming than credible. The past per se doesn't matter so much as do its remoteness and the demands its primitiveness makes on the imaginations of those inhabiting it: the slowness of letters; the wait to be endured after ordering a catalog item; the need to make up faces for the voices coming out of those radios. By setting *The Northern Lights* in 1959, Norman chose the last possible moment when a rural boy might become a teenager without having dialed a telephone or seen a movie. In making DeFoe a museum guard and Imogen a cemetery caretaker, Norman is making them walk in his own backward footsteps.

A story of Norman's called "Old Swimmers" concerns an aging character named Helen, the survivor of a long-ago ferry disaster. (In Norman's books, ferries are meant to sink, as planes must crash and zeppelins explode.) Helen explains to a nephew her reasons for marrying so late in life: " 'Because . . . Thomas, my fiancé, chooses to remember the same things I do.' " Even more tellingly, Norman has the narrator in "Jenny Aloo" declare, "My father told me once that the importance of any event was measured by your memory's loyalty to it. When he said that he was facing away from me at his work table, painting on a wing stripe."

A painter—of wooden birds or Dutch streetscapes or church murals—always has the chance to paint over a bit of his paintings. It's one more possibility in visual art that the writer, after publication, may envy. A reader must ask whether Norman, burdened with the irrevocability of both past and print, didn't conceive *The Museum Guard* with the sudden, possessed boldness of his heroes. Return to the author's 1989 collection, *Kiss in the Hotel Joseph Conrad*, whose stories are all republished here with "The Chauffeur," and you will find that the title piece begins in 1943 with a character named Imogene Linny. Could she, with her additional *e*, be the same Imogen Linny of the 1998 *Museum Guard*, who disappears into Holland—hopelessly, it seems—in 1938? Is her later/earlier life an extension/precursor of her earlier/later one? Which is the bird, and which is the decoy? Norman knows, and word artist that he is, he's not telling.

Previously published in *In Fact*: Essays on Writers and Writing (Pantheon Books, 2001).

THE CHAUFFEUR

THE CHAUFFEUR

MY ONLY CLIENT WAS MRS. MORO. WITH WHAT SHE paid me, I didn't need to drive anyone else. She lived at 1960 Jones Street, on Russian Hill, here in San Francisco. I live at 488 Columbus, Apt. 6-B, a few blocks up from North Beach. Every Tuesday, I picked her up at 6 A.M. In the almost two years she employed me, she was never ill or out of town.

The tableau soon became familiar. Mrs. Moro would be sitting on the dark red, wooden bench on the left side of her porch. I must say she looked childlike against the two-story brown house, with its tall door and slate shingles. It never varied, she'd be wearing cotton blue pants, a blouse, a sweater, and a black all-weather parka on top. This was her year-round attire. She'd either be sipping tea from a thermos, or holding the closed thermos on her lap. The few times she was asleep I didn't tap the horn. I simply kept the car idling until she opened her eyes, stood, smoothed both sleeves of the parka with her hands, took up her walking stick, and navigated down two levels of cobbled stairs to the curb. Naturally, I'd hold open the door. She was about five feet tall; she didn't have to bend much to get in. Then, I'd drive her across the Golden Gate Bridge, up Highway 1 past Mill Valley, out to Sir Francis Drake Highway, on through Inverness, and up to Point Reyes National Seashore, where she'd walk and bird-watch, rain or no rain.

Mrs. Moro was my patron, my driving companion, and, truth be told, one of the few people I had any sort of regular conversation with. And that was fine. Friendlier chauffeurs got extra work, word-of-mouth. I had Mrs. Moro, stuck with her, she stuck with me, and she paid me better than I could've ever imagined. Two people in a car for so many hours rely in equal measure on each other for things said and things unsaid.

Not that I hadn't had previous clients. I'd worked for Airport Limousine for five years before Mrs. Moro hired me. I was on call with a beeper. Mostly, I drove businessmen, airport to hotel, hotel to restaurant, to a nightclub. Waiting for a client on summer nights, I'd lean against my Lincoln Town Car, just looking at whatever street activity. Or sit in the car, reading one of my Joseph Conrad novels. Or Graham Greene. I did my book shopping at Clean Well-Lighted Place for Books. I had a small portable library in the front seat. It included some Italian authors, too; there was Elsa Morante, Dino Buzzati, Tommaso Landolfi, Natalia Ginzburg, my favorite. Whereas many of the chauffeurs I met at hotels, bar mitzvahs, concerts, weddings, and so on preferred music tapes to reading. I didn't have a single music tape. When my clients wanted music, I found something on the FM.

In this employment, I wasn't happy or unhappy, and it paid my rent. On occasion, I drove a stretch limousine, TV, wet bar, stereo system in the back, but I preferred the Town Car. In terms of human behaviors, life seemed less complicated with the Town Car. With the limousine, not often, but once in a while, there was lovemaking in the backseat, and then the awkward moment with the clients' mussed-up shirt or blouse, their extravagantly oversized tips out of embarrassment. Usually these were people who'd started out the evening all neatly tucked and tied, but ended up like a boozy scene in a film noir, or aspired to. From the get-go with my boss David Tallen, I refused prom nights or rich kids just out for a lark—you could tell by what my boss called their "on-phone demeanor." In a Town Car, there's no privacy from the driver, no privacy window, whereas in the limousine, there was, so in Town Cars the clients predictably acted in a more civilized manner. Only once did I ever say "Get another driver," and that guy was an out-and-out jerk, bully-the-chauffeur, obviously a show-off-for-his-girlfriend celebrity type, I think a weather channel host. I wasn't much bothered by it, really. I take things personally only from people I know personally. In that instance, I didn't even adjust the rearview in order to see his face after I'd dumped him back at his hotel. In fact, his girlfriend stayed in the car and I dropped her off at a party. Shame and embarrassment, just wanting to get away from the chauffeur, quite often resulted in hurried, over-sized tips. I'm just describing human nature in such situations. Let's see, oh yes, and one time I had Dustin Hoffman and his wife in the car. They were very polite and friendly and kept driver-client exchanges very cut-and-dry, which a driver appreciates. They went out for dinner, then to someone's apartment, then back to their hotel at 3 A.M. Generous tip that time, too. I worked for a pair of Buddhist monk dignitaries, the cellist Janos Starker, and, a year before he died, the famous deejay Wolfman Jack, and they are the extent of my name-dropping. Whereas some chauffeurs go on and on, like they became personal confidants in a few hours. "Yeah, Harold Robbins—the author? His wife always requests me." And like that.

Mrs. Moro, born in Tokyo, a bird-watcher and nice person, was anonymous, as far as I knew, to the world at large. She struck me as a very private soul, so I appreciated our conversations, some of which were only a few minutes long. On our fifth or sixth drive together, she said, "Tuttle Albers"—she always used my complete name—"Tuttle Albers, I have a present for you. A little gift. It's a book." She set a book called *Rashomon*, by the Japanese writer Akutagawa Ryū-nosuke, on the front seat next to me, then pronounced his name on my behalf. "Give it a try maybe." I read it while she was walking at Point Reyes, a murder story told from different points of view. When we started back to San Francisco, I said, "I read the book," and she said, "I'm pleased you read it so quickly. I know you did so because it was a gift, but I'm pleased just the same," and wanted to hear my opinion. In her questions, she was a bit like a schoolteacher, but I could tell she was enjoying herself. As usual, she fell asleep just as we got to the Golden Gate Bridge. I always had to wake her up when we got to her house.

To put it simply, working for Mrs. Moro got me out into nature. I mean that in two old-fashioned ways.

First, at Point Reyes, there was never an absence of hawks, and there were the smaller flitting kinds of birds, the usual crows. All sorts of ducks, Mrs. Moro told me, "abounded"— she used that word—in the lowland estuaries. There are maybe ten hiking trails at the National Seashore, names like Five Brooks, Chimney Rock, Mount Vision, Muddy Hollow. Some of the trails meander back before reaching the sea, but Mrs. Moro walked the same trail every time, the Estero Trail, which went all the way to Sunset Beach. "I take a quick nap leaning against a fallen tree," she once told me. "I believe it was struck by lightning."

Parked next to the Estero trailhead entrance gate, I'd do pretty much what I did when I used to wait for clients in the city. I'd sit in the car, or, weather permitting, lie on the ground and read. Or listen to KPXP Country. I had my Joseph Conrads, my Italians, and, as the weeks went by, the Japanese novels generously given to me by Mrs. Moro: Tanizaki, Kawabata, more Akutagawa, and a number of others. "No reason to expect you'd ever read in Japanese," she said. "Still, I feel sorry for you, that you cannot." In short, Mrs. Moro had provided me with my entire Japanese library. Remarkable as it first seemed, that a woman her age could make the three-hour trek to the ocean and back, after a few trips her stamina didn't at all surprise me. And she had her nap on the way to Point Reyes, at the beach, on the way home. Some days, after I watched her disappear over the hill, I'd drive into Point Reyes for lunch, even catch a noon matinee at the art house in Mill Valley, but I'd always get back in plenty of time. I made sure to tell Mrs. Moro my exact plans and wrote out telephone numbers, the car phone, the police, the movie theater, even the general store in Point Reyes Station. She kept these numbers in a small notebook. A separate notebook from her bird lists. "Birds are my greatest pleasure," she once said.

Turn left off Sir Francis Drake Road, go down a quarter mile of blacktop, continue along the hard-packed dirt road for another mile and a half, and you get to the parking area at the Estero trailhead. It's situated between dry grassy hills. In summer, there are dust devils, even an occasional brush fire; the National Seashore has its own volunteer fire department, men and women from Inverness, Point Reyes Station, and other nearby towns. Volunteers had VFD decals on wind-shields, lower left-hand corner. To either side of the trailhead, cattle grazed up close behind fences. I'd hear cattle lowing all day. And as I mentioned, hawks were always in abundance. Hawks were a constant. They'd be circling overhead, buffeted by the wind, they'd drift and rise on the thermals and swoop down into the crag gullies, and hawks were always patrolling the fields as far as the eye could see. I'd watch them but not study them, really, although I knew that Mrs. Moro studied them and even wanted hawks to be a common thing between us, because she gave me a field guide. "Hawks may be the easiest to tell apart. They're observable for long periods," she said. "However, the true test is shore-birds. To distinguish one sandpiper from the other has, for the twenty years I've walked the same path, been my nemesis. I have almost given up."

"Why do you keep walking to the same beach?" I said.

"Oh, that is simple. I hope to see white pelicans. I hope to see them. But why should they be in any hurry to let me see them?"

"Maybe if you'd come up here more than one day a week," I said. "I'll bring you up here for free, an extra time per week, if you want."

"That holds out the possibility of my not seeing white pelicans twice a week, instead of once. I don't think that would be a good thing."

Second, there was human nature. Because during Mrs.

Moro's walks to the sea, I would visit Grey Zamarkis, who was a resident research zoologist at the Tule Elk Reserve, out on foggy Tomales Bay, at the northern edge of the Inverness Ridge.

I looked this up in my appointment book, which I kept in my glove compartment: I met Grey the twenty-third time I brought Mrs. Moro to the National Seashore. I'd waited until Mrs. Moro drifted over the hill—the day was hazy and she looked a little like a mirage—and then I drove into Inverness to gas up the Town Car. I was standing next to the gas pump in front of the Inverness General Store when I saw this woman—I'm speaking of Grey, of course—putting air into the tires of her Land Rover. Not a candlelight dinner in sight, as the country-western song defined a romantic moment in a non-romantic setting. Not to leap ahead too far, but we ended up having country-western music in common; we made love to it and argued about it. For instance, one time I claimed that, although I enjoyed it, C and W basically promoted a drastically simple take on people. To support this, I cited a popular joke: What do you get when you play a country-western song backward? Well, you get your wife back, your kids back, your car back. "No, sir, uh-uh, nope," Grey said, shaking her head back and forth. "They may be drastic little soap operas, but they tell some basic truths about love and life. Just like great novels do. In less time, of course." Anyway, for the approximately six months Grey and I were together, we kept the radio on KPXP, and never changed stations, not in her Land Rover, the Town Car, or in her one-room "fisherman's hovel," as she called her rented clapboard structure at the end of a dock stretched out into Tomales Bay. Next to the Golden Hinde Boatel on Sir Francis Drake Highway. The dock slats were so unevenly rotted it was like walking on a long wooden xylophone; it made that many different hollow tones. Grey's rent was fifty dollars a month. She lived a twenty-five-minute drive from the herd of elk.

I met Grey on August 17, and later, as I mentioned, I entered our meeting in my work diary. I already had strong feelings for her, yet all I wrote was "Grey Zamarkis."

Standing at the gas pump, I'd noticed Grey's bumper sticker: I BRAKE FOR SASQUATCH. Now, normally, I'd have been repelled. Because driving as much as I did, I'd evolved an ever-narrowing tolerance for bumper sticker philosophies. I made it my obligation to disagree with each and every one of them, on principle. The principle being that any joke, platitude, Bible quote, political harangue, or ethical judgment that ends up on a bumper sticker asks you to be like-minded. But somehow, Grey's sticker didn't put me off. I felt generous toward it, willing to be persuaded that it declared that she was open to surprises in the natural world: should Sasquatch step out onto the road, she'd give it the right-of-way. I immediately thought of Grey as someone who'd defer to the mysterious. It's quite likely that all of this quick interpretation was based on the fact that Grey, at first glance and from that time forward, was so striking. The word "smitten" accurately applies to me, and I remember everything about that morning, including that her red hair was shaped into a tight configuration of braids, but was frizzed out anyway. When she stood up, I saw that she was taller than me by at least an inch; I am five foot eight. Though she was not a park ranger, a Smokey the Bear-type hat hung by a woven cord down her back. When she leaned over again to test the air pressure, the hat fell to one side. She got annoyed and flipped it back, and then must've felt me staring, because she turned and glared at me. She had a sprinkle of freckles along her nose. Since I thought she looked pretty elegant while just putting air in her tires, naturally I needed to watch her walk to the cash register, chat up the clerk, buy a pack of Neccos, go in and out of the ladies. And then I was both stupefied and pleased when she walked directly up to me and said, "Hate your car."

"Well, I'm a chauffeur."

She had a nice laugh. We had coffee while standing up in the store. Coffee and bagels to go. Conversation. Betraying no excitement. And two hours later, this was about 11:30 A.M., we were standing up in her open-top Land Rover, looking at a dozen or so tule elk. "I'm the only researcher in residence right now," Grey said. She handed me her binoculars and I looked through them at the elk. I could see that their noses were wet. I could see them scuffing up ground cover. I could see them nodding, shivering up along their thick necks, gazing in our direction, sniffing the air, nervously shuffling.

"We're in the elk's house—the Indians who used to live around here said—and some days, it feels like heaven to me," Grey said. "But I'll tell you what, elk can be nasty. They've gone for my vehicle. The reserve gets socked in by fog, mid-summer or not. And the forest—all these trees—can get like one enormous ventriloquist."

"How do you mean that?"

"Well, depending on the fog, how thick, how not thick, it's like an elk throws its voice. You hear one bellowing or coughing—it's more a chuffing bark—coming, say, from over to your left: But then suddenly the animal crashes right past you not ten yards away on your right."

"Could it be there's really two elk?"

"You don't get what I mean. Because you haven't experienced it yet. No offense."

"That's okay. We just met. I'm out here in my chauffeur's suit. These shoes. And these are the first elk I've ever seen, except for on Marty Stouffer's *Wild America* program."

"I hate that show."

"So do I—now."

"Yippee, our first thing in common."

Grey and I first started sleeping together two visits later. She had just turned twenty-eight that July 11, and my thirtieth birthday had been on March 14. She'd been married at nine-teen in Fresno, moved to Castroville, and gotten divorced at twenty-three. "He—that being Eddie—wanted me to be an artichoke wife," Grey told me, our first noontime in bed. "His family business was artichokes. All the women he was raised around and by became artichoke wives. They took care of the house, kids, did the books, et cetera. And I was that for four years of my life, Tuttle, right out of high school. Except that I had no children. I was derided for taking night courses at the community college. In biology. They were tough courses. And I mean derided. Sitting with family or friends, in a bar? My own husband, Eddie—he'd say, 'And what does our local intellectual say about that?' Whatever the topic. I think he was jealous because he read comic books and the occasional farm report, and there was TV. I'd married him, though; nobody put a gun to my head. Going from artichoke wife to zoology major was twice around the planet Earth, considering where I started out."

Grey was working on what she called her "late doctorate" in zoology, at the University of California, Davis campus. She knew a dictionary's worth of zoological terms, and had a nonplussed way of simplifying for me all the important theories in her field. She expected me to be interested, but didn't ask me to read any of the Ph.D. thesis she was writing. She was up-front about her need to budget her study time. I admired her constancy. Whenever I drove up to spend a weekend, I admired that she took her time in bed, too. And admired when she'd then get up, go to her desk, open her notebooks, and work until 3 A.M. If I was there on a weekday night, she'd get maybe two, three hours of sleep, off goes the alarm, she'd drink half a pot of coffee, and leave for the Tule Elk Reserve.

The working title of her thesis was "Predator-Prey Relationship Between Saber-toothed Cats and Tule Elk." At Davis, she'd studied with one of the world's foremost experts on sabertooth—the large, extinct cat that used to roam California—behavior. His name was Dr. Peter Volk. He was British, and had supervised excavations at the La Brea Tar Pits. Grey said he was demanding. He gave every single one of his graduate students *The Autobiography of Charles Darwin* for inspiration. He'd made sure that Grey steeped herself in all the paleontological writings about sabertooths, and she had to cross-reference that with predator-prey studies about other large cats of the world. "Partake of hours and hours of imaginative thinking and daydreaming," Volk said, "and spend as much time with tule elk as possible." One of Volk's theories—the one that excited Grey the most, actually—was that present-day elk might have a genetic memory of being hunted, say a thousand years ago, by sabertoothed tigers. She once let me read her notebook: "Passing the exams will be child's play, for you, Grey," he'd told her during an office appointment. "But if you want to make real discoveries, stretch your brain, get obsessed by far-reaching possibilities."

"At first," Grey said, "with all his talk about a poetic approach, I felt lost, and thought that Dr. Volk was patronizing me. That he didn't really think I had the scientific smarts. I mustered up the courage to confront him on this, and he said,

'I don't take just anybody into this program, Miss Zamarkis,' and that ended that discussion."

I admit I didn't grasp all of the ambitions of Grey's fieldwork, and very little of her thesis topic, but she made it sound exciting; I cared because she cared so much, and I told her that. She was dedicated. "I told Dr. Volk I was working long hours because I wanted to make up for lost time," Grey said. "He downplayed that. He said that, with a living animal—the elk, he meant, and then add this sabertooth deal to boot—you have to take your sweet time."

The first week in September I'd driven up on a Saturday afternoon to be with Grey. I got to her place at 4:15, and we were in bed by 4:30. That evening, we had dinner at The Station, in Point Reyes Station, a lively joint that specialized in Mexican. Grey was in a chatty mood. She'd gotten dressed up in a pleated, black Western skirt, a belt with a steer-horn buckle, a white cotton sweater, no bra, and a necklace of black pearls. And cowboy boots. She had her hair up in one braid, and otherwise it tumbled down, frizzy as it was. "Tuttle," she said, the moment we sat down, "I'm going to play the jukebox. I actually went to the bank yesterday to get quarters, hoping we'd be here tonight."

"We can go three doors down to Max's afterward to dance, if you'd like."

"I'd just as soon go home."

"That's fine, too."

"Or there's a movie, *The Lacemaker*, with that beautiful

Isabelle Huppert. Down in Mill Valley. My mother, I mentioned it to her on the telephone last night. She said she saw
it when it first came out, *The Lacemaker*, and that it had the
saddest ending of any movie she'd ever seen. The camera just
holds on a brokenhearted Isabelle Huppert's face for at least
three minutes. I said, Mom, you always thought that was me
in the school playground, you know, sitting off by myself
alone, and that's how I'd end up, too. But that was a movie
star sitting alone, jilted and forlorn, at the end of a movie,
not your own daughter, Mom."

"You just gave the ending away."

"It doesn't matter, does it? I mean, you only really experience the end by going through the whole story start to fin-
ish. A story's not ruined just by knowing the ending ahead of
time. Only a limited person would think that. And that's not
you, Tuttle. You're not in the least bit limited."

"Well, to a movie or back to your place. Either one's fine.
I know you like to work up your notes on Saturday nights.
Miss Lonely-hearts, huh?"

"I enjoy being alone sometimes, but not tonight. Tonight
I'm sticking with you. And I'm extra happy. Want to know
why? Because I felt like a sabertooth yesterday, all afternoon
yesterday. Usually, I try to imagine—like Dr. Volk suggested—imagine myself as a tule elk, a female. Nibbling grass
in the fog. Picking my way down to a rocky beach. You know,
get inside an elk's head. But two nights ago, coffee, coffee,
coffee, and the term 'predator-prey' came into my brain, and

17

I thought, *hmmmmm*, that I'd been one-sided in my concentration all of these months. So, yesterday, I was out at the range at 4 A.M., and I had a pretty normal morning. But in the afternoon—pow! I really got into being a sabertooth. It made a big difference, emotionally at least. Now, if I could only somehow get that experience down on paper."

The waiter brought our salads first, then enchiladas and Dos Equis beers. Grey ordered a pitcher of ice water, too; she was planning ahead for the spiciness. She'd ordered two chicken-and-cheese enchiladas, I got one beef and one chicken. When our food was all set out, I lifted my bottle and said, "May a saber-toothed tiger materalize right out of the fog, so you can see that."

We clinked bottles and each took a swig. "Talk about getting into someone else's head," Grey said. "You got into mine with that toast, Tuttle." She leaned over and kissed me. "It was a thoughtful toast. I mean that. Totally unselfish."

"Well, there's not too many people I'd be truly happy for, if something fantastic happened to them."

"I'm happening to you, Tuttle."

"Yes you are."

We ate and talked about this and that, and Grey played five songs in a row on the jukebox, which we could barely hear over the surrounding conversations. Finally, Grey slid her chair close up to mine. "How'd you actually choose your profession, Tuttle?" she said. "I should have asked sooner, I know." She turned beet red. "God, half a beer and I'm slurring. What a cheap date, huh?"

We both laughed, and I could tell by the directness of her smile that we wouldn't be going to a movie. In fact, my heart actually felt like it fluttered in my throat, and I wanted to leave the restaurant right then. But Grey was relishing her meal, she wanted to talk, as did I, really. All of which composed the happiness I'd have been loath to ruin.

"I didn't go into the family business, if that's what you mean?"

"I suppose I meant, what keeps you being a chauffeur?"

"Mrs. Moro—I told you about her. She keeps me in it."

"On the practical side, sure, Mrs. Moro pays you well."

"Not just the practical."

"You like talking with her about the novels and so forth."

"Plus, I admire her overall character, I guess is the way to put it."

"Obviously, though, she's a wealthy lady."

"I don't know for sure. I've never set foot in her house. It's an old house, old for San Francisco, at least. She told me it's the only one on Russian Hill that was designed by the architect Maybeck, very famous. One morning, I saw a man, much younger than Mrs. Moro, standing in the front window, and when she got in the car, she said it was her son, visiting from Tokyo. Maybe I'm wrong, but just the way she said it, she sounded disgusted. Yeah, probably she's very rich. I don't think my being her chauffeur's her only extravagance."

"You really really like her a lot, don't you?"

"In a funny way—and I'm not asking for violins. And present company excepted, she's turned out to be my one friend. Sounds unlikely, I suppose. I mean, she's sixty-seven. But, she trusts me to drive her. She trusts me to share books. In the car, we either talk or don't. It's nice for me. One time, it was raining cats and dogs, I said, 'Now, Mrs. Moro, you're not really going to walk down to Sunset Beach in this monsoon, are you?' "

"What'd she say to that?"

" 'Tuttle Albers—' "

"Sorry to interrupt, but your Japanese accent is atrocious."

" '—Tuttle Albers, my hope is to one day see a white pelican.' Then she got out of the car, put up the hood of her parka, and just started walking. She travels pretty light, the backpack, thermos of tea, maybe an extra sweater. Her walking stick, notebook, binoculars. That's about it."

"That's nice, Tuttle. I like hearing about her. I like hearing about you and her together."

"I didn't realize how much I liked her, though, till you asked."

"You probably just never said so out loud."

"I bet that's it."

We went to Baskin Robbins for an ice cream, sat on the enclosed porch. It wasn't crowded at all. We each got double scoops of vanilla in a cup. "Truth be told," I said, "I've lost my taste for driving. Not my knack for it. Just my affection. I don't have another profession in mind yet. I used to work for this guy, David Tallen, at Airport Limousine, and he was a good employer. I don't like working for anybody, really, but I didn't mind working for him."

"You must've run into some doozies. Clients, I mean."

"I'll tell you a story sometime."

"Tell me now, Tuttle. We're just eating ice cream."

"Yeah? Well, okay—this one time. David Tallen calls me up, he says, 'A Miss Banaktian—' this was about five years ago. David says, '—her mother and father are from Armenia. And they're flying in via New York for her wedding. She's a student at UC-Berkeley, and she's marrying a guy she met in school.' Okay—so these parents have never been to the U.S. I'm supposed to pick them up at the San Francisco airport, right? Then drive them to the Mark Hopkins. The wedding's that night at the hotel. Then the next morning, I'm supposed to drive them—a group—to Carmel, where they've got a house rented for a week. I'm supposed to wait a week, then pick them up, the airport, and they go back to Armenia.

"It's pretty cut-and-dry. And it's a nice job, because, one, since everybody's staying at the Mark Hopkins, I don't have to stick around for the wedding in order to drive them anywhere else that night. And, two, I get to see Carmel. And, three, I could take on other clients during the week. I did some addition ahead of time, and figured I'd come out with around six hundred dollars, plus a tip, but do you know what I ended up with? Three thousand dollars."

"How'd that miracle happen, pray tell?"

"I pick them up at the airport, and the future bride is in the backseat, and, Grey, she is very beautiful, very exotic-looking in a way. I couldn't understand a word they said in the car, but it was a teary reunion. The whole way to the city they spoke Armenian and laughed and looked at photographs from the old country and so forth.

"So. The wedding takes place. The next morning, 10 A.M. sharp, I'm at the hotel, standing by the stretch. A very sunny day. And out comes Mr. Banaktian, and he is looking highly agitated. He is not happy. I thought, hangover mixed with jet lag. I saw the rest of the family, aunt, uncle, mother, and the bride's brother, I think—and then I see the bride and groom. He's holding the bride's hand. But nobody—none of them—is looking in the least bit happy. I say to myself, 'You're going to Carmel. The seals. The sea otters. The beautiful scenery. Just roll the privacy window up, forget it, no problem. Down and back, it's the beautiful coast highway.'

"When all of a sudden, the father, Mr. Banaktian—he's about sixty—he comes up to me. His accent, mind you, is very thick. I say, 'Congratulations, sir. The bellhops will put your luggage in the trunk. I'm ready to go whenever you are.' I've already got the trunk popped open.

" 'Wait a minute—driver,' he says. 'Wait a minute.' I can't

do the accent. He says, 'Tuttle—' because I've got my name tag on. 'Tuttle, look. Look. Look, there, there's my new son-in-law, and what a piece of shit he is. My friend, my driver. I'm a *disappointed* man. This piece of shit she's married. Dirty. Dirty hair. And no job. He's what we call—' and he said something in Armenian. The words twisted up his face. 'He doesn't eat. At his own wedding banquet, he drank Coca-Cola—he's a fucking *string bean*.' " Grey was laughing. " 'You call it here, a *string bean*.'

" 'Tuttle'—and now he places my hand directly over his heart. He had a silk suit on, I think" '—you can't feel anything, can you, because I'm *dead*.'

" 'I'll get the bellhops,' I said.

"But now he grabs my arm tightly. 'Tuttle, look at my daughter,' he says. 'Look at her face. In her face is not a happy future.' Now he steps up close to me and whispers, 'Tuttle, my friend. In my country, I have position. I come from an important family. My mother, she's ninety-three. Ninety-three years old. She's seen a lot. She's been through a lot. She deserves peacefulness. A peaceful death. She controls the family money—you mention this to anyone Tuttle, my driver, and I will run you over with this big limousine, eh? I'm smiling. I'm smiling. It's my big joke. Relax. But, Tuttle, my American friend, my goodwill ambassador.' He takes out a wad of American hundred-dollar bills. He peels off two thousand dollars' worth, stuffs it into my suit pocket, and says, '*In addition* to your driving fee, Tuttle.'

" 'I don't understand,' I say.

" 'My mother,' he says, 'was too weak to come to America California for the wedding, her only granddaughter. I promised I would bring back photographs. We had hundreds taken. But no matter, no matter, because I promised her a special one, the bride, the groom, together—a photograph for enlargement—the groom stands next to the bride, eh? Tuttle, I look at you. I appraise you. You're a handsome man. I beg you—please.' He's actually got tears in his eyes. 'See that man across the lobby—our photographer. He's my cousin. He's going to take a picture of you next to my daughter. Just standing next to the impressive limousine. To my daughter, it will seem nothing, just a natural proud thing for her father, to show off the car, the driver. But I will personally see to it it is the only photograph of the bride and groom my mother ever sets eyes on, and she'll die in peace. Because you, Tuttle, are not a drug-head hippie string bean. Who somehow hypnotized my daughter.' He peels off ten more bills and stuffs them in. And he puts his face an inch from mine and says, 'To make my mother happy.' "

"And so," Grey said, "tossing chauffeuring ethics to the wind, Tuttle Albers accepts a whopping bribe."

"Weeks after it happened, you know what? I had very detailed, weird dreams."

"Such as?"

"It got pretty paranoid. See, this actual real event did happen, I *did* stand next to the Armenian bride in front of the

limo. The cousin snaps maybe ten pictures. I drive them to
Carmel and all the rest, no problems, no glitches, and I didn't
hear another word from Mr. Banaktian. All that was real life.
But then came these dreams.

"In dream number one, the ninety-three-year-old mother—"

"Oh, oh," Grey said.

"The old mother sees the photograph of me and her
granddaughter together, and she completely recovers from
her illness. She's all perky now. She's got the photograph on
the mantel, and Mr. Banaktian's put in a fix, and the bride's
not going back to Armenia so she can't say, 'That's not my
husband!' One day—this is my dream, now—the old mother
calls Mr. Banaktian to her side and says, 'I want to see my
granddaughter and her new husband. If you don't bring them
to me, I'll leave all the family money to a flock of crows.' "

"Crows?" Grey said, laughing.

"Grey—I'm just telling what I dreamed."

"Sorry—it's just that it's a Grimm's fairy tale, Tuttle."

"Anyway, that's dream number one. Dream number two.
I'm sitting home in my apartment. I've got my chauffeur's
suit on. I'm drinking coffee. It's late at night. The downstairs
buzzer rings. I say into the intercom, 'Who is it?' It's a sultry
voice with an accent—'It's me.' I press the buzzer. I heat the
elevator bell. There's a knock on my door. I open it."

"Of course, it's the Armenian bride," Grey said. "The
bitch."

"She's got her wedding dress on. Oh, my God. Oh, my God. She pulls the dress right off and gives me the deepest warmest kiss, then she says, 'The airplane is waiting.' 'Where's your husband?' I ask. 'Oh, it was so tragic,' she says." I took some bites of ice cream.

"So naturally there's a dream number three," Grey said.

"Dream three. We're living in Armenia, I've fallen madly in love with her. There's no turning back. We have children."

"Bad ending for me," Grey said.

"You asked me to tell this story."

Grey and I finished our ice cream. She ordered a cup of coffee. She looked at me, shaking her head back and forth. "God, Tuttle, you mean you and this bride—actually, *real life* now, might be in a photograph, in an actual house in actual Armenia?"

"I'm certain of it. This *actual* Mr. Banaktian wasn't kidding."

"If I see any Armenian license plates around Inverness, Tuttle, I'm going to get upset."

Grey went to the ladies' room. When she came back, I was sipping her coffee. She sat down and I slid the mug over to her. "I'm shifting subjects here," she said. "But, Tuttle, how much do you like your apartment? Because you really only have to be in San Francisco Tuesday morning and Tuesday night, Mrs. Moro up and back, correct?"

"Are you asking me to be up here with you more?"

"Not live with me. Not yet. My grant's only good for another year. I'm under a bit of pressure there. I was thinking, we could see each other maybe at least one, two other days a week. Or at least steadily weekends guaranteed. The Holly Tree Inn has excellent off-season rates. You could start out there—it's ten minutes from my place."

"She likes me. She likes me."

"You drive home, okay? I'm still a little tipsy."

I drove the Land Rover back to Inverness. Beautiful starry night. I parked as usual in the lot of the Golden Hinde Boatel. I kept the engine idling, the heat turned low. We were looking at a few scattered house lights in the hills across the bay. Grey started to use a fake Armenian accent, much more on purpose exaggerated than mine, "Tuttle, Tuttle," she vamped, "we make love on the dock. We make love like mermaids under the dock. My handsome American love ambassador–driver chauffeur Tuttle." She draped herself over me and we kissed for a long time, a real drive-in-movie make-out session, replete with steaming up the windshield. When we took a breather, Grey said, "How many children did you have with her." She wasn't using the accent. "I'm just wondering."

In Grey's room, we put on KPXP, "all night country, country all night," as the deejay said. We had a good time.

Over the next month, I noticed that the books Mrs. Moro gave me to read were either about suicide or edited, incomplete novels by writers who had committed suicide, according

to the "About the author" in back of the books. There was
Akutagawa Ryūnosuke's *Hell Screen, Cogwheels, A Fool's Life*,
which I found beautiful, but difficult reading. It was made up
of three stories. The third was called "A Fool's Life," and it
was like a diary. Each entry had a title such as "Laughter of
the Gods." Though Mrs. Moro more and more chose to sleep
and not talk, we still had animated conversations about the
books, if noticeably briefer ones. She'd given me the Akutagawa book on a particularly glum overcast and cold day,
which didn't help, or it might be argued was the perfect accompaniment to reading it. Mrs. Moro and I agreed—we said
this in quite different ways—that the writing was powerful
and disturbing (her two words), mainly about feeling puny
and useless. "It's none of my concern, Tuttle Albers," she said,
without a hint of sarcasm or even humor that I could detect,
"but I wouldn't suggest reading it out loud to Grey Zamarkis
in the bedroom." I glanced at her in the rearview mirror; she
shut her eyes and fell asleep, and did not wake up until we
were on Russian Hill.

Still, that day, Mrs. Moro had intrepidly set out along the
Estero Trail in the rain. I walked over to the telephone booth
and called Grey. The way I'd seen rainstorms lash the Tule
Elk Reserve, I thought she may not have gone into the field.
Besides, the night before, when I'd phoned, she said she'd
come down with an achy cold, possibly the flu. It turned out
she was at home. When she picked up the phone, I heard her
teakettle whistling in the background. "Oh, Tuttle, it's you,"

she said. "One sec, okay?" I heard her turn off the kettle. "I'm back."

"You sound pretty awful," I said.

"It's full-blown flu. I was really looking forward to seeing you."

"What're you talking about? I'm coming right over. The deli section of the Inverness store's got chicken soup, remember?"

"I already bought some. But I still feel lousy. I've got all this work, and it's slow-motion when you're sick, right? Energy's real low. But call me tonight, okay? Plus, I might be contagious."

"Did you call a doctor?"

"It's the flu. I don't have to call a doctor."

"Did you at least take your temperature?"

"It's 102.5. Temperature's only alarming data if it's 105. In between that and 98.6, I figure it's just the flu."

"I could just sit in the kitchen with you for an hour or two."

"Not worth it, really. Because if it's going to stay the flu a while, it means precious time away from the elk, too. So, you *know* I'm not doing too well, huh?"

"Poor girl. I'll miss you, Grey."

"Me, too."

"Okay, I'm hanging up then."

"Tuttle?"

"Yeah?"

"Why'd you call from a booth? Usually, you'd just drive right over."

"I was going to sit in the car and read a little. I figured in this rain you'd be working on your notes. But since last night you said you were sick, I wanted to check up on you."

"Sweet, and thoughtful."

"And. I'm worried about Mrs. Moro."

"Why's that?"

"It's hard to explain. She gives me Japanese novels, right? Well, lately, the ones she's given me—. I don't know. I mean, there's this author, Akutagawa."

"That's like a knock-knock joke. Akutagawa *who?*"

"The guy's a genius, he wrote a novel called *Kappa*, which is about spirit-amphibians, or something like that, but he makes them seem human—more real than people you see on the street. Anyway, Akutagawa killed himself. Mrs. Moro gave me what amounts to his fifty-page suicide note. Besides which, for the last two weeks, she's been sleeping most of the way up and back from the city. Whereas before, she might take a nap, but mostly we'd talk, too."

"She's allowed to be a little depressed."

"I'm not explaining it right."

"You sound upset, though. You just haven't thought it through. How much of her personal life does she tell you?"

"Not much. Two weeks ago, she mentioned that her son canceled another visit."

"Mother-son. That's always a possible culprit. Maybe it's the son."

"Butt out, is what you're saying."

"Sort of, yeah."

"She gave me this author Mishima—he's a suicide. Kawabata killed himself. After he won the Nobel Prize, too. Five out of five books she's given me in a row, the writer—each and every one."

"Is she out walking as we speak?"

"I said, Why not have a cup of tea at Point Reyes Station, wait and see if the rain lets up? But off she went."

"She's got sixty-some years' experience making up her mind."

"You don't think, just this once, I should follow her."

"Breach of trust. Or something like that."

"Okay. You're right. I'll phone you tonight then."

"Kisses to you, Tuttle. I feel like shit."

"Hope that doesn't last too long."

Mrs. Moro was coughing the entire drive back to San Francisco that evening. Every ten or fifteen minutes, she'd doze off, but coughing would wake her up. She wrapped herself in the blue thermal blanket I kept in a wooden box on the floor of the backseat. The box also contained a first-aid kit. I had a flashlight stashed in the glove compartment. I had a leather satchel for road maps. I had a state-of-the-art coffee thermos. In the trunk I kept flares. Anyway, the only thing Mrs. Moro uttered was so personal, I actually checked the rearview mirror to see if she was talking in her sleep. She was tented deep in the blanket, so all I could see was the top of her head, white hair. I heard her cough. But I could barely understand her hoarse whisper above the windshield wipers and rain on the roof. "Tuttle Albers," she said, "I've had the same dream for many nights in a row. I walk to Sunset Beach. It is raining. I've run out of tea. A beautiful flock of white pelicans is on the beach. One of them speaks in the exact voice of my mother, in Japanese. 'People at home want to see you—here, have some tea.' Then, like a magician, she makes a porcelain teapot appear. I taste the tea, but it is too hot and I singe my tongue, and it makes me wake from the dream." Mrs. Moro didn't ask what I thought of the dream. Telling it to me seemed to exhaust her and she fell asleep. She sank entirely down into the blanket.

The following Tuesday Mrs. Moro was not on her porch. This was so strange that I checked the date in my appointment book, then checked the front-page date of the *San Francisco Chronicle*: Tuesday, December 14. I idled the car and waited, heat turned on, until 6:45. Morning traffic had picked up along Jones Street, fog was thinning, and around Alcatraz tourist ferries were already out, and an oil tanker moved

32

slowly across San Francisco Bay. There was a cluster of sea-gulls on Mrs. Moro's roof. I'd always wanted to see the view from her window. Russian Hill was the section of the city I'd live in if I could afford it. I turned off the ignition and waited exactly another fifteen minutes. Finally, I drove to a magazine stand on Jones, parked, jumped out, and telephoned Mrs. Moro from a street booth. No answer.

I drove back to 1960 Jones Street. It was 7:30 A.M.

I stood on her porch, knocking. I rang the buzzer. Nobody came to the door. I drove to my apartment. I telephoned Mrs. Moro, letting it ring at least thirty times. I had a coughing fit out of anxiousness, I guess, because I knew, then and there, that if she could Mrs. Moro would've answered the phone. I telephoned her every ten or so minutes throughout the morning. I sat at my kitchen table and tried to read *Thousand Cranes* by Kawabata, tried to stay as calm and focused as his writing, and not obsess that Mrs. Moro had been mugged, murdered, or whatever other ambushes of city life. At noon I went to the Mission Diner, ordered the meat loaf, mashed potatoes, and coffee special, and called Mrs. Moro twice during the meal. Back at my apartment by 12:50, I watched daytime TV. The movie channel. *The 39 Steps*, directed by Alfred Hitchcock was on. I kept telephoning Mrs. Moro. Around five o'clock, I telephoned Grey and explained the situation, why I hadn't had lunch with her as promised, or shown up at all. I related Mrs. Moro's dreams to Grey.

"So, Tuttle, you think somehow she's, what—been called

home, so to speak? By her mother. I'm honestly trying to understand."

"Grey, I don't think *anything*. All I know is she wasn't on her porch. And she's not answering her telephone. None of this is familiar. None of it makes sense. My question is, shouldn't I call the police?"

"I'd leave a note on her door."

"What about hospitals? Last week she was coughing like mad. Like she might've caught pneumonia."

"Then call hospitals. You should call hospitals, Tuttle. Otherwise it'll drive you nuts."

"I'll drive up to see you as soon as I can."

"Okay. Keep me posted."

And in fact, I did telephone the five hospitals, public and private, closest to Russian Hill, plus a private clinic; none had an inpatient Mrs. Moro.

I got in the Town Car and drove to 1960 Jones Street. In my apartment, I'd written a brief note and found a thumbtack, and was going to tack up the note, then keep trying to call until I got through. But I decided to knock once more. This time, an elderly Japanese man opened the door. He was dressed in an elegant black suit, light blue shirt, black tie with a silver tiepin. "How can I help you?" he said. He had a tight-lipped smile, almost a grimace, and a serious, kind voice.

"I'm Mrs. Moro's driver," I said. "Tuttle Albers. She wasn't on the porch this morning so I could take her to Point Reyes, and I was worried."

"I won't invite you in. I'm Mrs. Moro's brother. Mrs. Moro died last night. Peacefully or not, how can we know? I flew in from Los Angeles."

I sat down on the wooden bench.

"I'm sorry," I said. "My condolences."

"You may sit as long as you wish."

"Thank you."

"Tuttle Albers. Yes, my sister spoke fondly of you."

"I'm very pleased to know that."

"You may sit as long as you wish."

"Thank you."

"Well, then. Please. I'll go into the house. There's arrangements. I'll be taking my sister back to Japan."

"I see. Of course."

"Goodbye then."

"Mrs. Moro loaned me a number of books."

"Books."

"Yes. Japanese novels."

"You read Japanese?"

"No, they were in English. In translation, I mean."

"I see."

"I'll return them."

"No need. Please. I must go inside."

"My card. My telephone number is somewhere in the house, I'm sure."

"My sister was very organized. I'll locate it."

35

"Goodbye, then. I'm very sorry. If you need to be driven anywhere—."

"No need."

I drove directly from Mrs. Moro's house and got to Inverness at 6:50. Grey was dumbstruck by my news. She made me spaghetti, but mostly we polished off a bottle of French wine. At about eleven at night, we were lying in bed. Grey had all sorts of new strength after her weeklong bout of flu. Across the room, her desk lamp was on, and on the table two candles were flickering low. Looking at the ceiling, she lay diagonally to me on the bed, her legs stretched over my stomach in such a way that I could massage her feet. "Maybe try and find another steady client," she said. "You can't replace her. I don't mean that. But the steadiness part, as soon as possible, might help."

"We spoke about you once," I said.

"You never told me that, Tuttle."

"The first time we—."

"Did what we just did, you mean?"

"Yeah—that morning, she'd given me a novel. By Kawabata, called *Snow Country*. Of course, I didn't do much reading that day. When Mrs. Moro got in the car, she noticed the bookmark. I had this fancy bookmark. It was only on page ten or so."

"Observant woman."

" 'You didn't stay interested in the story,' she said. So, I told her about you, partly to not hurt her feelings about the book. But mostly because I wanted to. Besides, she had an employer's right to know where I spent my afternoons. In case of an emergency."

"In case, sure."

"Another time, she said, 'How is Grey Zamarkis?' "

"You're pretty heartbroken about her, huh?"

"Heartbroken. I'm going to borrow that word."

"That's fine."

The next morning at 5 A.M. we sat at the breakfast nook table. We had orange juice, coffee, and toast. Grey was already dressed for the Tule Elk Reserve. I was wearing her oversized striped bathrobe. "I bought you a sweater," I said. "And I'm going to tell you something that's normally impolite. It cost one hundred fifty dollars, at Le Sweater. It's so rarefied an atmosphere in that store, when I bought your sweater, the clerk rang it up and said, 'Anything else?' One hundred fifty dollars plus tax, and she asks that."

"I like knowing the price. Maybe that's vice-versa impolite. Where is this mysterious sweater?"

I took the gift-wrapped box out of my overnight bag and handed it to Grey. She carefully undid the wrapping paper and put it on the table. She opened the box and lifted out the handmade sweater, black with a subtly pleated black pattern.

"It's really beautiful, Tuttle," she said. "And it's very feminine. You must be sick of my field duds, huh? Thank you, thank you, thank you. I was thinking just now: can we go to your apartment? Tonight, I mean. Can we drive down to San Francisco after I'm done working? I haven't been to the city in a year. I'd like to eat at Kupelos. It's the best Italian. I'd like to see your apartment, too."

"Fine with me."

"Of course, I'll wear this," she said, pressing the sweater flush against her chest, then fitting the sleeves against her outstretched arms. "This is so nice."

"It's a good color on you."

"I've got to get going, though," Grey said. She kissed me, a better kiss than the Armenian bride—that actual thought came into my head. She put the sweater on her bureau. "What're your plans for the day?"

"I brought one of Mrs. Moro's novels. I might not get out of this robe till lunchtime. Maybe I'll buy some new slacks and a shirt, Route 1 Cal-Mart. It's just a twenty-minute drive. I can't go out with you tonight looking like a chauffeur. We won't want to stop at my apartment first. I might even splurge on a new sport coat."

"You okay, Tuttle?"

"When her brother came to the door, I peeked around behind him, and I saw this hallway full of family photographs. It was a long hallway, with a wooden floor. There were five or six Japanese people sitting in the kitchen at the end of the hallway, too."

I made a quick sobbing sound, but it wasn't actually crying; events had just suddenly caught up with me.

"I don't have to go right now," Grey said. "Want some company?"

"You go to work. If I get lonely, I'll drive to the reserve."

Grey took up her day pack, kissed me on top of my head, and went out the door. I watched her until she got to the other end of the dock.

By 5:30 there was a light drizzle. The wind had picked up, too. I could hear ducks muttering under the dock. After she took a shower and put her hair up in mismatched braids, Grey put on the new sweater along with a black skirt, high, lace-up felt boots. She looked tremendously pretty. I had on gray slacks, white shirt, and a dark, herringbone sport coat, sleeves a touch long. In the car, Grey said that I looked nice, and I told her I'd spent $250.

"Between that and what my sweater put you back, you might qualify for the Living-Beyond-Your-Means Award," she said. "Or are you holding out on me, Tuttle?"

"I'm spending the rest of my meager savings at Kuleto's, too."

"Oh, boy."

"My apartment's not as bad as I might've hinted."

"Is there a bed?"

"Of course there's a bed."

"Is there coffee? Is there bread for toast?"

"We can pick up some bread."

"Money in our pockets. We're all set, then."

We were trying hard, in a mind-reading kind of way, not to mention Mrs. Moro. Grey knew I was pretty torn up over her. We drove along Sir Francis Drake Highway, south toward Route 1. It was about six o'clock, dusky light over Tomales Bay, and the rain had stopped.

"Let's start talking about Italian food," Grey said. "Naming different dishes. That'll guarantee we'll be starved for it."

"You know anything about Kupelo's menu?"

"I've been there twice."

"Oh."

"Don't ask."

"I won't. I'm just glad we're going, you and me."

"You could be a tiny bit jealous, if you want."

"You didn't go with Eddie. Not from how you described him."

"Not with Eddie, no. No, I went with girlfriends, actually. The first time. The second time, I went by myself. Anyway, I'll start: Penne with a perfect tomato and chopped mushroom sauce, accompanied by an Italian Chianti."

"That's what I'm ordering."

Just past Willow Point, at the southern tip of Tomales Bay,

Grey hugged herself and shivered. "Tuttle," she said, "maybe pull the car over, okay? You left the back window open."

"Must've been out of habit, to clear the air. Sorry."

"People don't think California gets cold—"

What interrupted Grey mid-sentence was a loud blur of white off the bay to our immediate left. Then the backseat was completely filled with noise. It was a squalling half cry, half-guttural moan, the combination of which was so bizarre and startling, I almost swerved the car. Grey somehow kept quite composed, though, and she swiveled around and said, "Tuttle, we've got a pelican in the car." As if to verify the fact, the pelican let loose a rusty pump-handle squawk, and I quickly pulled off to the side of the road. Grey and I both turned toward the backseat. The pelican was now hunched to the left-side corner. Its leathery-pouch beak was actually vibrating, clicking. "Jesus, *weird*," Grey said. "Interesting noises come out of that bird, huh?" The pelican feebly caped open its left wing, which drooped. "It might have a broken wing," Grey said. But then—the pelican lunged forward and I shouted, "Watch it!" Grey threw her hands up in front of her face.

Grey tumbled out her door, and I heard the splash of her boots in water. "Shit on a shingle—my boots, Tuttle, and I'm bleeding!"

Grey stepped from the shallow ditch and walked over to my side of the car. I was standing near the front bumper. She peered in through the front window, and her sympathies

41

shifted. "Guess what?" she said. "That's a white pelican. Rare to get them bay-side. They like the wide-open sea."

"Let me see your forehead a second," I said. I examined Grey's face, touched the cut and slight bruise on her forehead above her left eye. "I doubt you'll need stitches. I've got a first-aid kit in the backseat."

"Some uninvited houseguest, huh?" Grey said, and started to laugh. "I didn't see it coming off the bay, did you?"

"We got blindsided."

"Well, I'm basically okay, so we have to figure things out now."

"Let's go to the Point Reyes Walk-in Clinic. We should find out if pelicans carry diseases to worry about."

"I don't think it was the beak. I think it was the wing. It has hard, sharp wings."

"Just a precaution, Grey."

The pelican lifted and squawked, then beat its good wing hard against the closed window. It produced a mournful baritone gurgle, then rasping barks. "It's in pain, Tuttle," Grey said. "I think its wing is broken. I feel terrible for it."

I crouched along the car and opened the back door. Grey and I stood across the road. "Come out, come out, come out!" Grey said, but the pelican kept to the car. Every so often it fluttered its wing, half toppling, but its movements and distress calls had become half-hearted.

"This is pitiful," Grey said.

"How about the police?"

"They might shoot it."

"I doubt it, Grey. They might have a net or something. You must know somebody in Fish Game, or somebody else."

"Donnie Rush, the veterinarian's assistant! I've had coffee with her. Her boss is a large-animal vet, though."

"Come on, Grey, he's not going to turn down a pelican."

"Donnie'd be home, I bet. She has three young kids."

"And she'd contact the vet, right?"

"That's the idea."

"Okay. The Holly Tree Inn's a hundred yards from here. I'll go call this Donnie Rush. Is she listed under that name?"

"Rush, yeah."

"You stay with the car. I'll be right back."

A hundred or so feet up the road I turned and saw Grey toss her dress-up English raincoat over the pelican, then back away from the car.

The Holly Tree Inn had a pay phone on the porch. A phone book was dangling by a chain. I decided to call the veterinarian directly. I looked it up, and found a Dr. James Glass. I dialed and Dr. Glass picked up, which surprised me because it was after usual office hours, though maybe not for a veterinarian. I explained about the pelican. He said to try and put a sweater or blanket over the pelican to calm it down. "What about singing to it?" I said. "See what works," he said. "I'm only a few minutes' drive from where you are." He gave me exact directions and I ran back to the car.

We drove to the veterinarian's. He lived just outside of

Inverness, off Sir Francis Drake, up a winding road, in a house overlooking Tomales Bay. Grey's having put her raincoat over the pelican had in fact calmed it. On the way to the veterinary clinic, Grey looked into the backseat. "It's not talking," she said, giving a worried, nervous laugh.

The clinic was adjacent to the house. I ran up the stairs and knocked on the door. Dr. Glass answered right away. He was a tall man, about fifty years old, with the strongest-looking hands I've ever seen—wide, thick-fingered hands, not freakish by any means, no doubt hands comforting to an injured horse or cow, or a deer struck by a pickup truck. He walked down to the Town Car. Grey had opened the back door. Dr. Glass gently lifted the pelican, which was inside Grey's raincoat, and carried it up the wooden steps to his clinic. Inside, he set the pelican on an examination table. Grey and I stood against the wall across from the table. When Dr. Glass removed the raincoat, the pelican remained perfectly still. With slow, deliberate movements, he held the pelican firmly against his chest and administered a hypodermic. He'd had it filled and ready when we arrived. The needle made the pelican squawk open its mouth once, its only reaction. The air now smelled of fish. In a few moments, the pelican slumped like someone had cut the strings of a big marionette.

Dr. Glass began his examination. The pelican was anesthetized and Dr. Glass laid it down without its protesting. He lifted and examined each wing and leg, under its tail feathers, where he found a splotch of blood, and a little dripped onto the table. "Looks like a broken wing and some internal bleeding," Dr. Glass said. "We can x-ray right here. Fish & Game will rush an animal to Mill Valley Animal Hospital, if necessary."

He carried the pelican into the X-ray room, set it on the table below the machine, lowered the machine, calibrated it, turning two knobs. He then stepped into a small side room. Through the window, Grey and I watched the pelican get x-rayed. Dr. Glass then slid a thick metal plate out of the camera, if that's what you call it. We sat in the waiting room. Magazines were on the table. There was an aquarium with tropical fish in it. In about ten minutes, Dr. Glass stood in the doorway. "It's pretty well broken up inside," he said. "Internal bleeding, just as I suspected. A fractured left wing as well. It may be concussed. That's hard to determine. To be honest, this is my first pelican, and I'm not familiar with the literature. I had a heron in here two years ago. An owl sometime later. I think it's best to call Fish & Game, have it brought down to Mill Valley. That's my advice."

"How long will that take?" Grey said.

"Depends who's available. I'll make the call."

Dr. Glass went into his office. I saw four framed diplomas on his wall. Grey bent over, tilted her head, and looked into the aquarium. When Dr. Glass came out, he said, "Damn answering machine at Fish & Game. But I did reach Mill Valley Animal Hospital. There's a round-the-clock staff."

"We'll drive it there," Grey said.

"A good forty-five minutes, at least," Dr. Glass said. "I'll carry the pelican to your car. Keep the heat on. But don't suffocate it." He wrapped the pelican in a blanket. Then he helped Grey on with her raincoat; considering that the pelican had been inside the coat, and might well have bled on it, this was still so absentmindedly polite a gesture it made Grey blush and slightly stammer, "Thank you."

In the car, winding our way out onto Sir Francis Drake again, Grey said, "What we really need is a siren."

For at least ten minutes I was going well over the speed limit. But then, I'd guess four or five minutes south of Tomales Bay, the pelican died. We knew it had died, because it produced a classic kind of death rattle, which rolled up from deep inside its chest, unnerving kind of acoustics, really. It was the saddest sound I'd ever heard; Grey burst into tears, and that got to me, as well. We couldn't look at each other. I adjusted the rearview, and saw that the pelican looked like it was still alive, its eyes wide open. I noticed that Dr. Glass had fastened the seat belt around it.

Of course, San Francisco was long ago out of the question. I turned the car around in the parking lot of a seafood restaurant, and we drove directly back to the clinic. I carried the pelican up the stairs, Grey a few steps ahead. Dr. Glass was doing paperwork. He only had the small desk lamp on. He answered Grey's knock. "It died," she said.

"Bring it in," Dr. Glass said. "Just put it on the table, if you would."

I laid the pelican on the examination table, then joined Grey in the waiting room. "It doesn't surprise me," Dr. Glass said. "It took a hard blow. Pelicans fly pretty low and can build up good speed, as you know. Fish & Game will want an autopsy, even though it's clear *how* it died. The accident, I mean. There might be other information we can gain. Then there's taxidermy. For a community museum, or to bring around to elementary schools. Something along those lines."

"I understand," Grey said, as if comforting Dr. Glass. She was still sniffling and had swollen eyes. "I work at the Tule Reserve. Last spring, an elk slid off a muddy cliff. Fish & Game knew how it'd died but wanted it checked for all sorts of things, naturally."

"Yes, that particular elk was in my clinic, here. Small world," Dr. Glass said. "Look, you both seem upset. Can I get you a cup of tea? Or something a bit stronger?"

We both said no thanks.

"By the way, I'm Jim Glass." Grey and I each shook hands with him.

"There's nothing more to do, really," he said. "I'll take it from here. A little paperwork. That's about it."

"Thanks for your time," Grey said.

"Well, that's what I'm here for."

Grey and I didn't say a word driving back to her place. She sat at the kitchen table staring at her notes, or staring at the moonlight spread out on the bay, or putting her face in her hands, trying not to get upset all over again. We didn't have the radio on. I fell asleep on the sofa. When I woke up at 6 A.M., Grey wasn't there. I had slept in my new shirt, slacks, and sport coat. Grey's sweater and skirt were on the bed. Coffee was in the coffeemaker, and there was a note on the table:

> *Tuttle, darling. Needed to work. I just know you think the pelican has some connection to Mrs. Moro, but it doesn't. It was a sad freak accident. Don't be superstitious, okay? Hope you want to stay over tonight.*
>
> *Pals with you,*
> *Grey*

But I didn't stay. I drove back to San Francisco, and I don't know all the reasons why. I suppose I fled something. And I didn't visit Grey for three straight weeks, though we spoke on the telephone every night. We were very loyal to this nightly appointment. I'd call at 10 P.M. Grey would answer, "Hi." But, then, so much went unspoken, in fact most everything of real importance. What we should've said to each other was very, very close by, like the silences between tappings of Morse code. But we didn't speak it. Instead, it was, "How's the thesis going?" Or, "I drove a client today—yeah, I'm working, nothing taxing, though. My heart's not in it, really." The barest hints of our day. And after we spoke I'd drive around. And on Jones Street one night, I noticed a FOR SALE sign in front of Mrs. Moro's house.

One day, into the fourth week of not seeing Grey, I drove past a fairgrounds. They were dismantling the Ferris wheel. Across the field, two men were standing in front of an enormous helium filled balloon, like a zeppelin. The men were holding the anchor ropes, but at the same time, the balloon, with its gondola and bright lettering, was being deflated. I stopped the car to watch. I thought that the zeppelin might thrash about, act like a desperate, panicked huge animal when losing air like that. I'm not sure that seeing one thing caused the other, but I said "Grey" out loud, and then felt like my very breath had been knocked out of me.

Two days later, February 11, to be exact, I telephoned Grey, and instead of saying, "Hi," she said, "You thought the pelican was Mrs. Moro's ghost, didn't you? I've been thinking hard about this, Tuttle. I know we're not going to see each other anymore. Real Sherlock Holmes, huh?"

"Grey—."

"I'm going to a conference this weekend in New York. I'm not going to call you, and don't call me, either."

"What ghost?"

"That dream she told you. With the pelican, the teapot, the whole thing, Tuttle."

"Okay. Maybe it's been haunting me in some way. Maybe you've just articulated it."

"Good for me."

"Let's start this conversation over."

"No, no, you listen, Tuttle. You've been so distant. I mean, weeks of phone calls. We could've been—. You could've been at the Holly Tree Inn at least two nights a week. We were doing fine. We were moving ahead.

"You know what's scariest? What's scariest is when somebody you love makes a private decision, but he doesn't tell you what it is. And the result of that decision—the privately held conclusion—becomes like a ghost. It affects you deeply. It acts on you. But you don't get to fight back. It's very very very unfair, Tuttle."

"I haven't made any such decision, Grey."

"You haven't been here in a month. That's a decision. What we should address here, Tuttle—can you stop being such a fucking coward and own up to this? It's the pelican. After the pelican, something went wrong. It was bad luck is what it was, Tuttle. But you've purposely let us get estranged over it. You took it as some kind of omen. Look, I'm no shrink, Tuttle. I'm no psychiatrist. I've never been to one. But what I think—and I've been thinking a lot about us. I mean, I know you a little by now, right? You know what? Remember you told me Mrs. Moro was always hoping to see a white pelican?"

"That's what she said, yes."

"Well, she *didn't* ever see one, did she?"

"No."

"You liked her so much, didn't you? And you felt close to her. You wanted her walks to the ocean to go safely. You worried. When it rained, you worried. I mean, do you know how often her name came up in conversation? Very often. And I enjoyed hearing about her, don't get me wrong."

"What're you saying here, Grey?"

"I'm *saying*, Tuttle. What I'm saying. Is Mrs. Moro dying got to you. You felt she gave you things in life, Tuttle. I'm not trying to be sappy or philosophical, but she did give you things. Those novels. All that conversation. The sweet opportunities to worry over her. I don't know what all.

"So maybe—this is just a guess. Maybe, in your mind, you've turned Mrs. Moro into the one thing she most deeply wanted to see. Because that way she'd become her own good luck, the kind of luck she didn't have when she was alive.

"See? See, Tuttle? Her suicide was bad enough. Now you have to go and make it twice as bad."

"Her brother never used that word."

"Come on, Tuttle. It's me you're talking to."

"Since you've come up with such a complicated psychological theory, maybe you're the one who believes the pelican was a ghost."

"I'd be willing to have that in common with you, Tuttle."

There was a silence on the line then. "Look," she finally said, "I'm sorry. Probably my thinking's way off. At the time—

51

you know, when the pelican flew into the car? Between the two of us, I was the one most visibly upset. But since then, you've taken the incident and hoarded it from me, and you won't let me back in. Half the time, on the phone, it's been like we've just met."

We both didn't speak for another moment. I heard KPXP in the background, then heard Grey turn the volume down. "I hate this kind of talk," I said.

"Well, thinking about Mrs. Moro wandering some rainy beach was probably a torment."

"No, I meant us breaking up."

Grey gave a short sigh, then said, "This conference, Tuttle. It's all the bigwigs in my field. It's to interview for jobs. Research, teaching, you know, all the grant applications I've been typing. I bet you'll miss the sound of typing in the middle of the night, huh? Look up and see this naked girl typing. Anyway, I was going to grasp at one last hopeful straw, and ask do you want to come to New York with me, but I don't think it's a good idea anymore, truth be told."

"You'll be gone how long?"

"Probably a week. I have an open return flight."

"Which hotel?"

"I'm not saying."

"Well, it sounds mostly like a professional trip, a work thing, huh?"

"I might catch a Broadway play."

"Don't mind me asking. But do you want a lift to the airport?"

"The airport's got long-term parking. I'll drive myself, thanks."

"Just offering."

"I'm tapping my forehead, Tuttle. Tap, tap, tap. I'm tapping my forehead but pretend I'm tapping yours. Because I'm thinking, here I'm going three thousand miles away from Tuttle, but he's already—in his head—farther away than that."

Then the phone clicked down.

I kept on with my freelance chauffeuring, making ends meet, but not much more. As I said, my heart wasn't in it, but I didn't yet have the gumption to invent a new life. Then, eight months since I'd seen or spoken with Grey Zamarkis, she sent the newspaper announcement of her marriage to Dr. Glass. The envelope had the veterinary clinic as her return address. A month after that, a package arrived at my apartment. It was plastered with Japanese postage stamps. There was a customs receipt taped to the top. I opened the package on my kitchen table; it contained Mrs. Moro's bird lists. There were eighty-eight lists, in eight separate notebooks, all written in English, but with Japanese writing in the margins, too. Each entry was dated, along with the name of each bird, and time of observation, and brief description of where along the Estero Trail she had seen it. The official-looking letter that came with the lists was from the family's attorney. It was typed in Japanese, with the translation below it. Part of which said, "You are bequeathed. . . ." I knew that Mrs. Moro had employed drivers previous to me, to take her to Point Reyes. I hoped that I was the only one who'd been willed her bird lists.

I put the lists in my desk drawer. Another week passed, and I decided to drive up to Point Reyes. It wasn't anywhere near the anniversary of Mrs. Moro's death; it wasn't a morbid kind of sentimentality or anything. That is, I didn't want to try and please her ghost. I just wanted to see if I could remember the names of hawks. It was a crisp, sunny day, no traffic to speak of when I set out at 10 A.M., and I made good time. I got a coffee at the Inverness store, then drove up Sir Francis Drake, past Grey's cottage—well, it was no longer hers, of course, and she never called it a cottage. I turned left and drove the few miles to the Estero trailhead sign. The glassed-in display held a few stuffed birds and mammals, paintings of local flora, a list of proper trail etiquette, a warning about deer ticks, with an enlargement of a microscopic tick, and a dotted-line map of the Estero Trail.

I had on jeans, tennis shoes, a flannel shirt, a sweater, a parka. In my backpack, I carried a thermos of water. I had binoculars around my neck. I had the field guide in my pocket. In two hours, I was able to identify two kinds of hawks with certainty, but I didn't really care about anything, except to look at them. I got to Sunset Beach. It was a pebbly, wide curve of sand, zigzagged with shore-birds, dozens of them scurrying along the edge of the froth, like they were stitching each wave to the beach with their beaks. Though I knew that they were trying to find something to eat. I sat on the fallen tree. I took up the binoculars and scanned the horizon. Brown pelicans—I knew that bird. And seagulls diving just out past the whitecaps.

I stayed for an hour or two, I guess. I ate the tuna sandwich I'd packed. I drank some water. I may have dozed off for half an hour or so. When I woke, the sun was a sharp glare. Chill wind, sun, a clear view of the sea. I thought a moment about Grey. I missed her. I didn't forgive myself about her, didn't forgive myself in the slightest. Every worst maudlin C and W song would've wholly captured my stupidity and regret, then multiply by ten. "Sadness in severe disproportion to the opposite," as Akutagawa wrote. Other than about Grey, I don't remember what I thought. But I know this: what fixed me in that present time and place was my deep happiness at not seeing white pelicans. I was hoping that I wouldn't. This was my first time. They might've been indignant, knowing I hadn't earned such good fortune.

Kiss in the Hotel Joseph Conrad

THIS IS A STORY ABOUT MY UNREQUITED LOVE FOR IM-
ogene Linny, which began in Halifax during the war and is
still going on.

In June of 1943, I was a celebrity, for good and not-so-
good reasons. I was in jail and I was in the papers. It was a
case of small things leading to big damages.

One morning I was taking a rookie through maneuvers
out over the Atlantic. That was my job, to train pilots. It was
instead of going overseas. His name was Junkerman—Haj
Junkerman, a nice enough kid, redheaded, married with a second child on the way. Earlier that morning his wife, Teal, sent
me a pineapple upside-down cake. She must've heard about
my sweet tooth. Junkerman was embarrassed, but what else

could he do but hand it to me, the two of us standing there in the locker room, him holding the cake? I took it and said, "How about let's have some of this once we're up in the air?"

He got a quizzical look, but he wanted to please, so he said, "Should I get forks from the commissary?"

I put the cake in my locker and said, "On second thought, let's have it when we get back."

It was the first day of summer hot enough to fill the beaches. Droves of people came out to Peggy's Cove. Their brightly colored towels we saw from the air. Junkerman and I were about ten miles out when I got the urge to invent an emergency. Naturally, there was no sense to this, none at all. I was an expert in the basics, but I guess there was a giddiness in my character that made me fool with the training manual. The rationale I concocted was that an unexpected crisis would challenge Junkerman and keep me on my toes. But in truth such moments just spiced up the air time. Colonel Mc-Clernan, my commanding officer, had chewed me out more than once for this type of behavior. He said I was reckless, plain bad luck. The bad luck part stuck in my mind the longest. But the RCAF was short on instructors, so I took advantage. Besides, the greenhorns liked to fly with me.

So Junkerman and I were out on this clear summer morning, when I flipped on the intercom. "You see that smoke?" I said.

"No sir," he said. "No, sir, I do not."

At which point black smoke began to pour from the left

engine, because I'd shut off an oil line. Then I took the plane into a sharp tilt followed by a double spin. Now, to an experienced pilot with a clear, mechanical way of thinking, the smoke and the acrobatics probably wouldn't have seemed related, but to Junkerman they obviously were because he whimpered, "Holy Jesus." This inspired me to aim the plane toward the beach. A fire the size of a horsetail flared out of the engine.

"Don't mind the instruments," I ordered Junkerman. "Just keep a finger on the ejector button and whatever you do don't panic."

"Jesus, Jesus, Jesus," he said. By then I'd caught some nerves myself, almost forgetting I was the one who'd caused the arson in the first place. Of course by then it didn't matter because we were really in trouble. I lowered the plane, wobbling it for effect anyway; as long as we were going down I wanted to put on an air carnival. The beach at Peggy's Cove came into full view, and as we dipped and veered, all the beachcombers, swimmers, and loungers scrambled up toward the road.

"We have a choice to make here," I said through the intercom. "We can bail out, let the plane go where it will . . ."

"But, sir . . ."

"Don't interrupt me, Junkerman. Or: we can ditch in the ocean."

"Sir . . ." Junkerman was a sincere kid. "Sir, we can't hit the beach, sir. All those people!"

"You've got morals, Haj. The thing about me is, I don't." Then I blew a loud sigh through the wire into his earphones. "Have it your way. Say a prayer."

"Jesus, God," Junkerman said.

It must've looked spectacular from the beach, and for us it was a wild ride. The ocean came at the windshield, then the long bouncing skid, a wave peeling out from each side, and then we were at a standstill, except for some bobbing. I'll say this for Junkerman, he rode it out, but almost the second we were down he ejected. Rocking the plane, the hatchtop catapulted free, Junkerman shouting, "Whoa!" and he was gone. A bit stunned, I imagine, he floated in his life jacket, which was tucked high under his arms, before circling in a frantic dog paddle. Junkerman was splashing like crazy. Right away the lifeguards rowed out, a pair in each of three wooden boats. They wore rubber bathing caps, their oiled shoulders glistening in the sun. Their oars were rising and falling in unison, it was like a parade on the water.

I hoisted myself out onto the nose of the plane. The small whitecaps ricocheted bright snaps of light, so I kept on my sunglasses. When the lifeguards got closer, I waved my helmet by its leather strap. Hundreds of people were waving back with towels like signal flags, but I couldn't hear a single voice except for Junkerman's. "Here! Over here!" he was shouting. The lifeguards picked him up first. I was pleased to have the extra time to collect myself. I remember it as a peaceful moment. A reckless thing was over.

There was an inquiry, and in the newspapers a psychiatrist put my character in doubt. The plane was towed to shore and went through a check-up that revealed no essential defects. "Such hard, overwrought flying in the service of training pilots sometimes does mysterious damage," is what my court-appointed lawyer said, though I didn't know if he was referring to me or the plane. Junkerman was all but mute on the witness stand, loyal to me even though he'd been duped up in the sky that day. He sat up stiff and jittery on the witness chair, and during the hearing he wouldn't look at me. "He saved all the people on the beach," is all he offered, even to a yes-or-no question. So to me he was the hero, though in reality neither of us was. Haj Junkerman never spoke to me again.

The prosecutor called me loony, but loony or not, I'd caused Canada embarrassment, he said to the reporters that came around like sharks. A couple of newspapers ran opposite headlines: PILOT AVOIDS TRAGEDY ON BEACH! and AIR FORCE PILOT FALSE HERO IN FLIGHT SHENANIGAN. Both headlines rang true.

While the court-martial tribunal deliberated, I was kept in jail. Fan letters came pouring in for the entire month, along with threats and marriage proposals. The guards got a big kick out of reading my mail to me. Finally I was acquitted, mostly thanks to Junkerman's testimony, since he was the only witness to the actual sabotaging of the plane, other than myself. And on the stand I'd lied.

The morning I got out of jail, I was given civilian clothes and taken to the colonel's office. "Your tour of duty is over," he said, spitting into a wastebasket. It was just me and him in the room. "You aren't being honorably or dishonorably discharged. We've come up with a new, Asshole category, personally speaking. But for the record, it'll be like you were never in the air force to begin with. You're a ghost to us."

By the time all the paperwork was done, it was evening. The colonel's assistant drove me in a jeep to the Halifax wharf, said, "There's lots of rooming houses around here," and dropped me off. I stood for a minute or two in the street, not knowing where to turn. Then I took out my wallet, checked the amount of money I had, and walked into a camera store, where I bought a camera and some film. This was my new life, and I thought I'd take some pictures of it.

I wandered along the Halifax wharf until I came to a kissing booth set up to raise money for the war effort—one dollar a kiss. Mostly air corpsmen were on line. Some mock-saluted me and said things like "Way to go, buddy," nodding their heads like they pitied me. I just stood there, shuffling along as the line moved, looking ahead to Imogene (I didn't know her name yet) in a booth makeshift as a kid's lemonade stand.

Imogene looked about my age, which was thirty, though maybe she was a year or two younger. She had a white flower in her black hair, and each time a man stepped up she'd lean forward and pucker her lips. After each kiss she'd take a tube of red lipstick and brush it across her lips. Between kisses she looked bold and shy at the same time, a provocative combination, if you ask me. Even if I wasn't concentrating so hard on her so as to ignore the razzing, Imogene still would've been a vision of surrender to me.

I finally got close enough to read her name tag and see her blue eyes. She wore a pale green summer dress and white high heels, and her pocketbook sat on the counter next to the lipstick.

The voices around me just faded away. I was happy to be out in the balmy night air, happy to be out of jail and a few steps away from Imogene.

When I got to her she recognized me. "You can kiss something," she said, "but it ain't, I guarantee you, my lips."

This remark sent laughter all down the line. The men right behind me snickered. "Fall out, flyboy," one guy said, and he roughly slapped me on the back.

At least Imogene had the decency to hush them down. Then she looked at me and said, "I was on the beach that day, and if you'd of killed me with that lunkhead stunt, I'd of never forgiven you." She placed her hands on her hips, and I noticed she wasn't wearing a wedding ring. Then she reached out and snapped the dollar bill from my hand. "Next!" she said. There was nothing I could do but walk away.

I retreated some yards away and took a snapshot of Imogene just as she leaned forward for a kiss.

I then went to the arcade and found a booth where you could get pictures of yourself taken. Inside under some clear plastic were pictures of other people laughing, frowning, and making faces, which served as an example of what you might do. I sat down, pulled the curtain shut, slid my coins in, and pressed the button. In a minute and a half I had six pictures. That night I found a rooming house, Twin Oaks, on Robie Street. The proprietor there, an elderly woman named Mrs. Black, asked me what I did for a living, and I said I was between jobs. She said if I was still situated as such in two weeks, I should look elsewhere for a bed, and then she asked me for two weeks rent, thirty dollars.

The next day I took my film to the camera shop to be developed. A week later I picked it up. When I got back to my room, I cut out the snapshot of Imogene and pasted it to a photograph of myself, so as to make it look like Imogene was about to kiss me. I tacked them up on my wall. I knew it was a crude fantasy, but it gave me hope.

I was broke, so I had to work at a fish-processing plant. Salmon, cod, bluefish, perch, and sea bass. It was my job to scrape off their scales. Fisheries and canneries employed a lot of ex-military. The foreman didn't like me, I could tell at first glance, and I was worried that my reputation would keep me from getting hired. But then he shrugged and said, "Working here, at least you won't run a plane into the cannery." Every weekday I spent long hours alongside a conveyor belt, in line with other cleaners. My apron was splattered with scales, guts, and blood, all of it used for fertilizer. The smell of dead guts choked my nostrils.

Six months went by, during which time I found out that Imogene was dating a hotel owner named Szymon Szechter. I don't know how they met, maybe on the street one lucky day, or even in the kissing booth. Anyway, he'd given Imogene a job as manager of the Clark, one of the three hotels he owned in Halifax. I'd sit over there in the lobby, happy to get a glimpse of Imogene as she walked into the hotel's restaurant for lunch or stood behind the front desk, speaking to a clerk, looking all proper and businesslike. And there I'd be, with fish scales under my fingernails, my face mostly hidden by a newspaper.

My salary was barely enough to pay room and board. But luck had it that I found a moonlighting job as custodian at the Union Hall. Every Friday night a dance was held there.

The hall was on Barrington Street, near the wharf. I'd arrive on Friday at about seven o'clock, and the hall would be empty. The first thing I'd do was go into the men's and women's rooms and provide each sink with a bar of scented soap. Most fishery employees worked overtime, even on Fridays. They'd arrive at the hall straight from the plant. The dance hall had scented soap so that all evidence of fish could be washed from their hands and faces.

After I supplied each sink with soap, I'd polish the hardwood floor. I used a long-handled machine that had two round brushes. It hummed along nicely and reminded me of a land-mine sweeper. Then I'd set out fold-up chairs along the walls, and the four refreshment tables needed to hold stacks of paper cups, bins of ice for soft-drink bottles, a coffee machine, and sandwiches. There was beer, too. Hot dogs and hamburgers got delivered later. I'd place a chair and table with a 50¢ ADULTS sign near the entrance. That's where the ticket taker sat.

Pretty soon the musicians meandered in one at a time, wearing secondhand tuxedos. I liked these men, but had no idea what their lives were like outside the hall. I knew about their needs at the bandstand. Jaques Cozry was the trombone player, and he had a bad back. He used a special cushion that I kept in my locker. The band leader was named Louis Kammerer, and he started the evening with a lime-water-tinged whiskey. These requests were my connection to the musicians.

They were a close-knit bunch; almost never argued except once in a while when Case Danning, the lead sax player, broke in on Edison Kruse just when Edison cut loose on piano. Or sometimes he'd do it when Jaques's solo went on a little too long in his opinion.

Once the band's needs were seen to, my custodial chores ended. I'd go to my locker and put on a suit and a new pair of socks. Every Friday I'd buy a new pair, my reward for getting through the week. I'd walk onto the dance floor, drink a beer, maybe two, but I wouldn't eat so that the beer'd work up to my head faster. I liked to dance and would've been happy to spend the evening with any number of partners, though I had my favorites. Karen McClelland was one, tall

Abigail Luard was another. I always hoped they'd show up, because I could say to each of them, Let's spin around the dance floor, and they'd say yes.

Here is where Szymon Szechter, the hotel owner, comes back into the picture. Even when it appeared she was tired or suffering from a cold, Imogene arrived promptly at ten o'clock, arm in arm with Szymon Szechter, like a queen. I knew that Szechter had investments in the processing plant and in the canneries. That's why he was allowed in the hall—stockholders, union members, and their families and friends all came to the dances. Szechter always wore a black tuxedo with a white carnation in the lapel. By the end of the evening the flower would have traveled to Imogene's hair.

Szechter was vain. He was his own applause. His every gesture seemed to offer himself congratulations. Now, I'm sure people were impressed with him, what with his being handsome despite that pompadour haircut, which wasn't too distinguished for a man nearly fifty, and that mysterious name, Szechter, which made anyone who pronounced it correctly seem like his personal friend. His photograph was on the society page almost every Sunday; Imogene usually stood in the background. As for me, I formed an opinion at first look, and my opinion got more heated every time. I didn't care how many hotels he owned, how many islands he'd been to, how many tango and waltz lessons he had as a kid, or what kind of big-shot sedan he drove. I considered him just right for a postage stamp honoring the great cemeteries of Canada.

Don't forget, even though Imogene and I only had that one sour talk at the kissing booth, she was my heartthrob. You can imagine how my brain sizzled whenever I saw her with Szechter. I'd just have to sit down, even middance.

I took everything about Imogene personally.

One day, the strain of this unrequited love became too much, and I left Halifax. I quit both my jobs just by not showing up, packed my clothes, my snapshot of Imogene, and took a train to Calgary, out on the plains, where dog racing held some promise.

First thing when I got to Calgary, I made sure that the hotel I picked out wasn't owned by Szechter. It was called the Frisch Hotel. The front desk clerk was a friendly lummox named Bix Houghton. "No, a Mrs. Malouf owns this hotel at present," he told me. I said I'd be asking the owner's name now and then. Bix handed me my room key and said, "Fine, that's your privilege." I unpacked, washed up, then had meat loaf and potatoes for lunch in the hotel restaurant. Then I hitched a ride out to the dog track at the outskirts of the city. It was an indoor track with betting booths under the grand-stand. High at the top of the grandstand were private glassed-in suites.

After looking around, I went to the employees' office and got a job exercising the greyhounds and helping out Dr. Tus-itala, the vet. That mostly involved holding down injured dogs while he gave them sedatives, examined their ribs, or put on splints. If the dog was snapping, I'd muzzle it. Whenever there was an accident, I'd go right to the vet's office. Every so often the dogs would spill over each other, their legs all tangled, dirt clods flying every which way. Usually a few dogs kept after the rabbit, but most just stood still, heads bowed, tongues lolled out and panting. A track attendant would then herd the dogs through a gate, while the track was smoothed by a special wide rake attached to a pickup. All the bettors got their money refunded.

But mostly I sat around with the grounds crew. We'd listen to American baseball games, when we could pick them up. We heard the war end on the radio. We talked about our problems and complained about wages, and things just went along. After work I'd sit in my khaki uniform, with my plastic employee's pass pinned to my breast pocket, and eat in the hotel's restaurant. Usually I'd go to a dance hall at night. I still kept to dance halls and hotel lobbies, so that even though I was in Calgary I was my old self.

I worked at the dog track for six years, until 1950. But my life never centered on the track, or the dance halls, or hotel lobbies, for that matter. At night, I'd lie awake thinking of Imogene; until I fell asleep, when I'd dream of Imogene. Her life with Szechter was like a Parisian boulevard, whereas mine was just a nameless alley.

But my work at the track wasn't a misery until one September afternoon when Imogene and Szechter showed up there. I'd read in the newspaper that they were coming to Calgary. Szechter wanted to purchase a hotel or two "on the frontier." What's more, the paper said they were getting married in a private train car at night, by candlelight. They'd be sightseeing, touring the cities. They'd be staying in hotels that Szechter bought along the way. After reading all this, I checked with Bix to make sure the Frisch Hotel hadn't been sold. "No," Bix said, but he saw me clutching the evening edition. "But *that* Mr. Szechter, however you say his name, he sent an agent on ahead. He's made inquiries."

One crisp autumn afternoon, the newlyweds and their wedding party arrived at the track. Photographers trailed behind them, and they made their way up the stairs to their suite. A lot of spectators recognized Szechter. A hotel man was a big deal back then, especially since Szechter had already been photographed for magazines with American movie stars.

I quit during the fourth race, saying to Rudy Severance, my buddy on the grounds crew, "Rudy, I'm gone. Don't forward my mail."

Rudy knew just what I meant. I'd told him all about Imogene. We shook hands. Rudy winked and said, "Good luck with every minute from now on, eh?" He smiled, then headed toward the greyhound pens.

I fled Imogene in Calgary, but went right back to Halifax, where she still made her home. This time I rented a room in the Hotel Joseph Conrad, a five-story brick dive on Bolange Street. It was in a part of town where even from the top floor you couldn't see any of Szechter's hotels. The view was of loading docks, a tugboat wharf, Quonset huts, and farther out was Halifax Harbor. The name? I learned that the hotel's first owner, Alix Quonian, had a thing for Joseph Conrad's novels, a fetish I'd call it, since she had the hallway walls papered with pages of Conrad's books, a different novel on each floor. Maybe she dreamed of going to sea. Occasionally, tourists dropped in, wanting to see the room where the author slept or the table he wrote a book on. I heard one ask Arnie London, the desk clerk, "When did Joseph Conrad live in Canada?"

Late one night—it was my fortieth birthday—I got drunk and slurred through some sentences of *Nostromo*. The book's cover was displayed in the glass case where the fire extinguisher was kept. I'd never read anything by Joseph Conrad before. That night I read maybe a whole chapter, I don't know. I was shouting, carrying on like an actor. This was on the second floor, but nobody opened their door to tell me to pipe down. Maybe they liked being read to.

Besides its curious name, the hotel didn't have much to offer posterity. The joke was that more people had checked in than had checked out. The register at the front desk was filled with scribbled signatures. Transients, mostly, and old tenants who signed in each night just to make sure they were home. On winter days, people drifted in off the street to sit in the lobby. The big radiators there kept the lobby warm as a bakery.

My room was 411. It cost twenty-eight dollars a week, and my finances being what they were, the hotel remained my address. Our three bellhops lived there, too. Their names were George, Maxwell, and Emory. The youngest was Emory, fifty-eight when I moved in. None of them would carry luggage. One worked the elevator, while the other two played poker at the corner table in the lobby. They saw their cards by a tall lamp that had a frilly lamp shade. They'd play all afternoon and half the night. They'd doze off on their chairs. They seldom wore their square caps or escorted new patrons to their rooms. They no longer represented the old courtesies.

You could tell by the chandeliers that the Joseph Conrad had once been a very grand place, and the lobby still had plush red couches and the original tables. There were maids, but they didn't even dust the bannisters.

I had a surefire way of finding work, which was to keep my expectations low and never make work the most important thing. It couldn't be; there was still Imogene. I got a job as a shortorder cook, breakfasts and lunches only, in Lambek's, the coffee shop down the block. It had a sign shaped like a huge coffee cup with a swirl of steam rising out of the middle. On a plate alongside it was a doughnut.

I'd kept track of Imogene in the papers. I knew that she'd returned to Halifax, and I kept clear of her. But I couldn't forget her, either. Then, after eight years of the same life, I realized I was losing touch with things. There was no hope with Imogene, no encouragement. My life felt shabby. I felt on edge, delinquent toward every hour.

The neighborhood outside the hotel was changing. There were new faces, new languages, new bakeries. But I felt locked in the past, shackled to it. I went whole breakfast shifts, month after month, without saying a word. I went weeks without talking, except maybe a nod to Arnie London, or I'd sit in on poker games, muttering bets. I was associating only with people in the lobby.

I turned forty-five.

Then a curious thing happened, which I followed in the business section of the *Chronicle-Herald* night after night. I noticed that Szymon Szechter had begun to sell some of his hotels. There was no overnight collapse, but I felt in my gut that Szechter was going under. Dwindling luck began to show on his and Imogene's faces. I examined their pictures with a magnifying glass. They weren't smiling as much. I read a lot into every one of their expressions, and to me they looked insulted by twists of fate. Though I have to add that Imogene looked as beautiful as ever.

A country can get tired of one man's luck and turn against him. At the time it was hard for the average family to get a mortgage on a house, yet here was Szechter, with all his hotel rooms, thousands of roofs over his head, saying things like "I like being famous because everyone knows which hotel I run off to for privacy," and signing five-foot-long cardboard checks at charity balls. A lot of people looked at that and shook their heads, I bet.

For me, a hotel corridor has always been a neighborhood.

75

You hear sobbing, whispering that's louder than talking, doors slamming, meals eaten in the small hours, radios, and you have people so lonely that they forget and leave the DO NOT DISTURB signs on their inside doorknobs.

In 1962, Szymon Szechter died bankrupt, and shortly after a friendless funeral—the hearse, one limousine—Imogene Linny moved into the Joseph Conrad, so that my unrequited love was living directly across the hall, in 412. Her presence there told me all I needed to know about how miserly Szechter's will had proved. I took it all as a stroke of personal luck.

I'll describe our reunion, if I can use that word without implying any affection on Imogene's part. She'd been in the Joseph Conrad for just less than a month and still wore a turned-down black hat with a black lace veil, though I thought she mourned for her own life more than for Szechter. In the hotel everyone left her alone.

One evening, as I read the newspaper in the lobby, I looked up to find Imogene standing directly in front of my chair. She was then near fifty, with all the looks she'd had in the kissing booth but add twenty years to them.

"I've seen you," she said. "In this lobby. And going up to your room. You never take the elevator, do you?"

"I'm sorry to read about your loss," I said. More than sorry, I was flabbergasted to find her standing so close.

"Thank you," she said.

She lowered the veil over her face.

"Want to sit down?" I said.

"No, thank you," she said. A few moments went by. "I remember your face," she said. "You're that stunt pilot, aren't you? That careless man who nearly killed me on the beach. I'm correct, am I not?"

"You took that far too personally," I said. "It was dumb, I admit. But you weren't in any danger, not really."

"I take everything personally," she said. "Why not? What else is life for? I take this conversation personally. And you should take the fact that I've remembered you at all quite personally."

"Believe me, I do," I said. "I do."

"Very well, then," she said. "Good night."

As she turned I said, "You know, Mrs. Schectner"—she didn't correct my pronunciation—"I've found out that Joe Danurand, he's the proprietor here, I've heard that Joe's about to retire. They'll be looking for someone. And I thought, what with all your experience . . ."

"I have a little saved," she said, "which is no concern of yours."

"Well, maybe you'd want to hang on to it," I said. "A rainy day, and all that. 'Course, you're right, it's none of my business, but maybe a paycheck wouldn't hurt. You were a working girl back when I first met you."

"*Met* me?" she said.

"Well, back in forty-three, remember, I paid for something

but never got it." I could tell right away by the look on Imogene's face that what I'd said disgusted her.

"You fool!" she said. "Your brain's a buzzard house. Men were dying—that's why I worked in that booth. There was a war on. But what would you know of that? You were the town dunce back then and probably still are, because people like you don't change, do they?"

"If you have an opinion, don't hold back," I said.

Imogene reached into her black pocketbook, rummaged around, and took out a dollar bill. She crumpled it up, then tossed it at me, and then she took the elevator up to our floor.

Still, there was hope. Joe Danurand told me that Imogene talked to him. He said, "She knocked on my door and asked for the job. She said she had good references. I said, Who can vouch for you? She looked at the floor, and you know whose name she came up with? Yours. She said it like she didn't want me to ask who else, because there might not be anyone else. Anyway, I thought it over and went to the higher-ups and the job's hers."

As proprietor, Imogene won't allow drunks, loiterers, or hookers, and she put a sign in the hotel's front window using those exact three words. She's got a heart for such people but tells them to get lost. "I've got a reputation to uphold," she said one night after refusing a room to someone. Maxwell, still a bellhop, was standing there and said, "You meant the hotel does, don't you?"

A little wounded, Imogene looked right at Maxwell and said, "Yes, I supposed that *is* what I meant."

Every week for a year I asked Imogene out for coffee.

I think it was my persistence she finally took into account and allowed me one visit a week in her kitchen, for a little small talk.

"Do you think talk comes easier before or after a cup of coffee?" I asked once.

"I don't think about it," she said. "I don't think about the same things you do."

That sort of conversation.

The other evening, at her kitchen table, she said, "That kissing booth. Boy, was my mouth sore." She said it as if remembering only to herself. "Like I'd been sucking on lemon rinds all day."

This year, my rent went up ten dollars a month.

Whether I'm cooking eggs or sitting in the lobby with the bellhops, the photograph remains tacked to my wall. Imogene has never seen it. In the photograph, my face is the exact same distance away from hers as it's always been. While a few other things in life have changed, that hasn't.

I wash my face. I knock on her door. Sometimes, Imogene isn't all that happy to see me.

JENNY ALOO

"SSS—SST! HEY, OLD DOG. WOMAN DOG. DOG, PISS ON this box. Crazy dog woman go head piss on it!" Eskimo kids yelled. Hard talk right at her face; but they never laid a hand on Jenny Aloo. I saw all of this because a jukebox was on the loading dock of the Churchill train station, where I was in charge.

One boy spit. Jenny wiped it off the jukebox with her hand. This was in December 1959. Each morning she'd tidy up the jukebox—the first jukebox ever in Churchill. She'd chip ice from its buttons with an ice pick kept in her jacket. She'd breathe on the hard-to-reach deposits until they melted. She'd have nickels with her, a parcel of food.

"Piss on it!"

"Hey, don't say such," Jenny said. "That's an *uncle*, in that box."

Falling-down laughter; blank pain on Jenny's face.

The kids, some her nieces and nephews, had caught on to her routine. When they saw her coming they'd form a half circle guarding the jukebox, legs locked together like a group wrestling match had begun. Then Jenny would have her pick, pull at her hair, witch her way through. A few would back off in mock fear, hooting, hissing. A girl kicked the jukebox. Intent on clearing away every last grain of ice, Jenny'd ignore them. She wouldn't spin around angrily, spit, or give chase. Instead, she'd calmly slip a nickel into the slot.

She couldn't read the names of the songs. It didn't matter. She'd close her eyes, punch the buttons, and wait. One time, country western. The next, a pop star, Buddy Holly, Elvis. The short, mechanical arm lowered a black platter with a mouth that spun; a happy voice, a sad voice, no difference. The thing was, she thought—*believed*—her son, Moses, was trapped inside the jukebox! Imprisoned there by a malicious sorcerer. She knew such men still worked their terrible magic, had evil talents and used them for their own satisfaction. People like her son became victims.

We serviced one train line: Winnipeg-Churchill. Every Tuesday and Saturday, the Muskeg Express arrived at 7:05 and departed at 5:35 in the evening. There were two trains: one with a big Maple Leaf emblem on its caboose, the other with a CNR, Canadian National Railroad, decal on its caboose. Along the way were about a hundred stops. Of course, some towns didn't have a depot. People just knew where to wait. Engineers told me that they'd sometimes see an arrangement of suitcases beside the tracks, stop the train, back up; when they'd hear the train, families would appear out of the woods.

I was nineteen and had been stationmaster for a year. Elias Sutton had the job before me, until his retirement at age seventy. I had been apprenticed to him for eight months, and he never made it easy. Elias didn't much like me, said he couldn't like me, because from just those few months I'd gotten knowledge of invoices, crates, and luggage that had taken him forty-some years to get. "What's fair in that?" he asked. Not only did he hold me responsible for the unfairness, he refused to discuss it. I'd been warned that Elias put a lot of energy into grudges, against both the dead and living.

By the time he handed me the duplicate office keys, he was frail, nearly blind. Most of his strength seemed to reside in his bristling white hair and temper. That day, he acted surly and clasped his own set of keys as if their weight kept him from blowing away in the wind. Wind, as I recall, not as fierce as it often got in town. We stood near the train. I smelled the steam and friction.

It was awkward. We kept glancing about. His face was set hard, eclipsed of sentiment. "Toby Sprague," he said to me, "this job is *ours* now. It's just you the company's seen fit to pay for doing it."

That same evening, Elias asked Lloyd Rowley, a local brakeman, to put a couch in the office. "My retirement villa," Elias said, pointing to the ratty piece of furniture. For six months, eight, ten, long after I had found the knack of things, Elias prowled around. I thought hard about how to ignore him, but my thinking failed. He snickered; judged my work harshly out loud. His coffee maker remained off limits to me. I brought my own coffee to work in a thermos. His mail was sent care of the luggage room. That was an odd twist since the hotel he lived in was just down the street. He kept a game of solitaire going at all times, so I seldom sat at the only table.

Two years later when I left Churchill for good, Elias took his old job back. I handed him the keys, "Wore you out, eh?" is what he said.

In early 1958, the year I was apprenticed to Elias, my parents left Churchill for Halifax, where my mother's ear specialist was located. My mother, whose name was Grethel, was born in Canada of Swedish parents. She had a "mental disease of the ear," at least that's how my father put it. This meant it was a sort of hypochondria that finally resulted in true ailments. Mother did suffer. Actually, she had two specialists in Halifax; again, as my father put it, "one for the ear part, one for the mental part." Now and then, Mother would have spirited fits of worry that her doctors talked about her behind her back. "Considering what I pay them," my father said, "they should talk about *nothing* but you!" They made four trips a year to Halifax, for five years. Each trip required five days on a train, one way. "The fact is," my father said, "your mother prefers to live near her doctors."

That was part of why they left. The rest would make a long list of dissatisfactions. My mother's feelings of isolation seemed doubled by my father's inwardness. My mother would often pack a suitcase in the middle of the day. I'd come home to find her slowly unpacking, meticulously placing blouses, stockings, sweaters, and shawls in drawers and closets, as if she were moving into a new home. Or perhaps the hotel where they stayed in Halifax.

My father's name was Abel Sprague. His was an unusual business. He designed and built model planes from scratch, in a small, cluttered workshop in our apartment. He made up pilots' autobiographies, which he included with each model in his catalog. One time he built a plane called the Lesser Antilles Barracuda. I asked him if the Lesser Antilles, islands he showed me on a map, had an air force. "They do now," he said. The silver plane was sleek, slit-windowed, with a barracuda's grin decaled under its droop nose. Before he sent it to a customer in Vancouver, my father read my mother and me his lengthy composition. It began: "A hurricane held the islands in a death grip, the first time I took the Barracuda out." He signed it with the pilot's name.

We'd moved to Churchill from Toronto when I was ten. My father reasoned that having his planes sent from Churchill would give an air of mystery to the whole enterprise. No one, he thought, knew anything about Churchill, except that it was far away. All his business was mail order, of course, but this proved unreliable. Model planes, no matter how expertly packed, could arrive damaged. A broken plane meant weeks of work lost.

One morning my father and I carried three of his tightly packed models to the airstrip at the outskirts of town. It was an ominously windy day. Gale-force gusts swept in, moaning through the streets, leaving an uneasy calm. My father paid the government mail pilot, Dane Hibbit, ten dollars to secure the models behind his seat, away from the heavy mail sacks. But as the plane taxied, the wind swerved it, and after a few comical hops on the runway, a gust slammed the plane down hard enough and at such an angle to anchor it. We ran out, my father muttering, "Son of a bitch," over and over again. Dane Hibbit had been thrown clear and lay on the ground holding his ribs and laughing in a hysterical way. When we got to him, he said, "A month's leave with pay," then blacked out.

My father began sifting through the scattered cargo, interrupting his search only to go over and kick the plane. "Son of a bitch," he said. "Junkheap will be flying again in a week— but *my* planes!" Then he saw his packages. He approached them slowly, then sagged to his knees. Dane Hibbit groaned awake. I watched my father unwrap his planes, the paper flying out over the tundra. Three men from the air terminal arrived, out of breath, and once they saw that Dane Hibbit was alive, they also watched my father lifting out each splintered plane. He held one up, waving it in the air the way a child might, pretending it flew in windy weather. I walked over, afraid to get too close. Yet my father looked surprisingly calm. "I think it's best," he said, concentrating on the plane, "to move to Halifax soon. I'll open a shop there. Near the wharf. So that in summer, I'll keep the windows open. Hang the planes from wires. From the ceiling, you know?" He kept moving the plane back and forth. "Your mother would like that, don't you think?"

"Yes, I do," I said. He seemed in shock, as if he'd been in the crash, and he muttered to himself as we walked home. Early the next morning, things were back to normal and he'd started his repairs.

I have no photographs of my parents. By and large the memory I have is an affectionate one, though I can't for the life of me recall how they looked. I've worked around that, though, by focusing on other things. I can still see my father's work table, the stacked blocks of balsa to be whittled, sanded, balanced into his aerodynamic masterpieces, sawdust rings where his coffee cup had been, the smell of glue.

Being stationmaster wasn't a difficult job, though it kept me busy. I've already mentioned invoices, crates, and luggage, which didn't take much resource. Then there was the office, which had to be kept orderly, the address tags, wire mail baskets, and ledgers all in place. It wasn't a life's work, just one of the steadier jobs available. Most men my age had already gone to work elsewhere, for government agencies or the army, though some had stayed put, and of those, many had begun to drink.

Churchill had two hotels, a post office, an Anglican church, a hospital, the train station, all at the edge of the tundra, on the shore of Hudson Bay. Winters were god-awful long; six, seven months, and they could bury your heart's longing for the rest of the world or make it fly wildly around the frozen streets. Each train arrived with a thousand miles of snow on its roof.

North of town were enormous chutes and bins where grain was stored. Churchill was an important part of the northern trade route. Throughout the summer and early autumn, Polish, Italian, and Japanese sailors were in town. The last ship, Polish, always left by October to avoid treacherous ice. Once, I played soccer on deck with some Polish sailors and accidentally kicked the ball overboard. It flew out and hung in the air like a planet.

Along the Churchill River, between the grain docks and town, was an arrangement of squalor shacks called the "flats." The crosswinds there were famous. They had a piercing, cold dampness, an unceasing commotion. One night, I watched from my apartment as Jenny's son, Moses Aloo, came reeling drunk out of the shack he and Jenny shared. He was carrying a lantern. There was a large, bright moon, and it was possible that he'd intended to gas up his boat and set out to a good hunting place, hoping to reach it by morning. His boat's motor was propped up on sawhorses. With an unsteady hand,

Moses picked up the gas can and tried to empty some gas into the motor's spout. Then, he stumbled and the lantern smashed. A line of flame advanced toward the motor, which Moses had knocked to the ground as well. Moses rolled away as the motor exploded.

I saw the explosion but didn't hear it, for the winds took the sound in the opposite direction, or held it suspended near the shack. However it worked, it wasn't a trick of memory, it was the winds in the flats.

By the time the jukebox arrived by train, Moses had been missing for a few weeks. His absence had been noted by store-keepers, police, and friends alike, and everyone was on the lookout. Moses was a rough man, but likable, though when he was drunk he'd find his gun and shoot it at the river. On occasion he'd worked at the station, unloading baggage cars, but did that only for pocket money and otherwise didn't like to work for anyone. I thought I'd seen him walk from town early on the day he didn't return, but Jenny claimed he'd slept late, and his cousin, Thompson Aloo, said he'd talked to Moses that afternoon in the grocery store, and that Moses had shared a cigarette with him. But I could've sworn it was Moses I saw, carrying his rifle. It was around seven o'clock, and I assumed he was going out after rabbits or ptarmigan, winter game. He was on the road out of town, which was potholed but straight as the landing strip.

Then, on December 3, I was attending to some freight, which included the jukebox. I recall the exact date because the jukebox surprised me so much that I double-checked its invoice. Two men helped set it down on the loading dock, then went in to the waiting room, with its dozen hardwood pews and big radiator at either end, to have a smoke. There were usually Eskimo people who'd sit for hours in there, and not necessarily waiting for a train. It was just a good place to meet, talk, and sleep. Jenny went to the waiting room each morning during Moses's absence to ask after him. I'd watch her approach, with her off-center way of walking, tilted slightly to her left. She was, I'd guess, sixty, squarely built, just under five feet tall. She usually wore a shapeless dress with a rope belt, leggings, and a faded denim jacket over two, sometimes three sweaters. And black galoshes, their buckles jangling. Her round, red-brown face was windburned, her eyes tense. When she inquired about Moses, she'd sound angry. "Moses been here?" she'd say, close up to someone's face, like a challenge.

The morning the jukebox arrived was no different. I was sure that she'd made her rounds; the two-machine Laundromat, the church, the post office, the grocery. Then I saw her crouched between freight cars, watching Elias and me.

"Invoice says Montreal," Elias said. "In Montreal, there's bars people dance in. This jukebox got here by mistake."

Elias, who wore a greatcoat, striped railroader's gloves, knee-high rubber boots, and a stocking hat, took a rag from his pocket, then wiped the curved glass clean. He read the instructions. Over his shoulder, I saw that it said five cents a play. Elias put his curiosity to work right away; fetching an extension cord, he plugged one end into a socket under the desk, the other into the jukebox's plug. "Holy damn," he muttered, "forgot nickels." He returned to the office, trailing the cord there and back through his hands, as though he needed it to find his way. His eyes were so bad that was possible.

Elias pressed his face to the glass. "Let's see who wants to sing to us," he said, pushing me an arm's length away.

"Hey!" I said, thinking, Stubborn old coot. Technically speaking, the jukebox was under my jurisdiction, and I could've said so. Instead, I clenched my fists, sucked in my breath, and let it out thick as smoke into the chill morning air.

I knew that Elias was using his frailty to bully me, that he was clingling more fiercely than ever to the stationmaster's job I now had. Still, this was the first jukebox in Churchill, so I allowed that Elias should have the chance to work it.

His face an inch from the glass, he silently read the song titles. "My," he said, "my, my." He put in a nickel, pressed a letter button, holding it down a few seconds, then a number button, which he let pop right back up. Frank Sinatra sang "Come Fly with Me." Elias clapped his hands like a magician scattering doves. Then he took off his gloves, placing his hands on the glass as though it gave off heat. The song ended. He put in a second nickel. "Now," he announced, "B-three." He pressed the buttons. I looked over to see Jenny still crouched between train cars. She held that pose through the next song, "Blue Moon," then walked over to us.

"What's this?" she said.

"A jukebox," Elias said.

"Whose?" Jenny said.

Elias looked at me. "Mine," he said, "for now. It got here by mistake."

"If it's a mistake," Jenny said, "you don't want it eh? Give it to me. I'll take the mistake home."

Elias grimaced, shaking his head. "I said, it *got* here by mistake," he said sharply. "You can't have it."

"It's lost, then," Jenny said. "It can live with me."

"I give up," Elias said.

"What was on that coin you put in?" Jenny said.

"A five," Elias said.

Elias brushed past me on his way to get a third nickel, then tripped over a sack of laundry I'd left near the table.

"You'll kill me yet," he said.

"I'll get it out of your way," I said. "I was just going to take it over to the Laundromat. Be back in a short while."

"Don't matter to me if you come back at all," he said. He walked to the jukebox.

I took up the sack of clothes and walked head-bowed against the knifing wind toward the Laundromat, which was across a dirt street from the Tundra Inn, the three-story hotel where Jenny cleaned rooms six days a week. Behind me, I heard a mutt squeal and snarl. I turned around to see Jenny kick it out of her way.

"You following me?" I said.

"I want to know about that box," she said.

"Not much to know," I said. "Elias took charge. Probably he'll do some paperwork on it. Then, say in a few weeks, he'll send it on to Montreal, where it's supposed to be."

"Thought you were the boss now," she said.

"I am," I said.

"Then you tell Elias something," she said. "Tell him that box didn't get here by mistake."

With Jenny close behind, I stepped into the Laundromat. Five elderly Eskimo women were packed together on a slat bench, in front of a dryer tumbling one shirt.

"Hello, Toby Sprague," Ruth Omik said to me. Ruth's husband, George, worked the gantry crane and was my warehouse foreman. Ruth wore a kerchief around her dark, wrinkled face.

"The washer's free," Ruth said. The Laundromat seemed filled with these women, though even without them it would've been cramped. The dryer and the washing machine faced each other with barely enough room to squeeze by in between. There was a table to fold clothes on, squares of cardboard under two of its legs. Under the table were baskets that fit inside each other. The window was steamed over.

Along with Ruth was Sarah Omik, her cousin; Mary Nuniviaq, also a cousin who was visiting from Padlei; and there was Mary Oopiaq and Philomene Nuqac. All these women were about Jenny's age, dressed in worn coats over jackets, sweaters, and dresses, with thick woolen socks tucked into galoshes. In town, I'd seldom seen Ruth without Sarah, Mary Oopiaq without Philomene. They'd be together in the grocery, the station's waiting room, church. They'd all known each other since childhood.

It was midmorning and they were having a meal; small chunks of fish and fat had been laid out on paper towels on their laps, and a bottle of whiskey was being shared. They kept their coats buttoned to the top, as there was no other heat.

Ruth stood and took the shirt from the dryer. Then, like a sitting bucket brigade, the women passed a basket of laundry down to Ruth, who emptied it into the washer. "Some others are on their way here soon," Ruth said to me. "Better put your clothes in." I did that, then saw Jenny move directly in front of the women on the bench.

Her face was jittery and she rocked on her heels, looking like she wanted her friends to ask, "What is it?" yet knowing they'd wait. Their restraint was tuned to hers. They knew it had something to do with Moses. What else could it be? But as-yet unspoken news of Moses's whereabouts would be handled with the same delicacy as news of his death—for all they knew, Moses might already have turned up dead. Maybe that's what Jenny had to tell them. Maybe he'd been found along the tracks. It wasn't unknown for someone from the flats to be discovered like that; he could have gotten drunk, walked all day from home, then just sat down.

For a few minutes, the women talked around the subject of Moses.

"Last week," Ruth said, "I left a little fat in a pocket. Pocket of a shirt. Had to wash it twice."

"I did that once," Philomene said. "Only it was trousers. And it wasn't fat. Some chocolate."

When the dryer stopped, the silence was deepened.

Then Jenny stammered, "*Jukebox*," working her mouth over the syllables as if they were hard candy. "A jukebox," she said, "got here by train. It's a box, full of songs. A five-cent. You put one in, a song comes out."

"Go on," Ruth said.

"It's Moses inside," Jenny said matter-of-factly.

I stared at Jenny, hardly able to comprehend what she'd said. But not one of the women so much as winced. They nodded solemnly. For them, it was all a matter of concentration, of gauging how deeply Jenny believed that she'd located her son.

"When did it get here?" Ruth asked.

"This morning," Jenny said.

"Whose is it?" Philomene said.

"Elias Sutton said it got here by mistake," Jenny said.

Ruth stood, opened the door to the dryer, fluffed up the socks, trousers, and long underwear, then closed the door and put in another dime. When the dryer started up again, she motioned for Jenny to take her place on the bench. Jenny slumped, locked her fingers on her lap; her mouth was tightly drawn, her eyes closed. The metal snap on a pair of trousers kept tapping the oval glass. "Toby," Ruth said, "we're going to talk in Eskimo now. It's easier to figure things out that way. Figure which evil man did this, to Moses. Because look—look at her face, just look at it. Her Moses, he's in the box. That is the truth."

Then they had a conversation.

Workmen such as George Omik had told me about sorcerers, direct, factual-sounding stories without, as far as I could tell, embroidery of any kind. Stories with a lot of detail and told with conviction. And in them the things sorcerers did were wild, unpredictable, violent.

Around 1900, one story went, a man appeared carrying a spiral narwhal tusk, pointed as a harpoon. He gathered everyone in town, then demonstrated his immortality by sticking the entire tusk through his chest. "This is *nothing*," he said. "You get me angry, you'll see. This is nothing." There was no blood in evidence; the tusk stuck out straight as an oar. He yanked it out and allowed spectators to run their hands over his chest in amazement. Two men who voiced their doubts about the sorcerer's authenticity were later found stabbed to death. A decade later, another sorcerer appeared (a few people recognized him as the same man) in the guise of a sixteenth-century priest. He was a living mockery of Christianity, however. Tongueless, he uttered loud, indecipherable monologues in front of the Anglican church, scaring most parishioners away. He harassed women, kept his filthy dogs inside the church, and one day simply disappeared. So: there were stories, and probably down the line this one, with Moses in the jukebox, would be added to them.

The others left, but Jenny sat saying nothing.

I zipped up my coat. "Toby," she said, opening her eyes. She sounded short of breath, as though in a daydream she'd been slogging through snow. "Toby," she said insistently, without a trace of pleading. "I need you to do something. Come home with me."

I can't say why, but I didn't hesitate. "Yes, okay," I said. "I'll leave my clothes here."

"In a basket," she said. "They'll be safe."

I walked close behind Jenny toward the flats, across a snowfield littered with bottles, sections of track, stray shingles blown off shack roofs. It was snowing heavily, but I could see black smoke rushing out of tin chimneys up ahead. The wind was up, tearing the smoke into rags.

In front of Jenny's shack, the mutt was whimpering; being kicked must've made it think it belonged to Jenny, or maybe it did. Opening her door, Jenny kicked the dog inside, where he circled in a corner near the woodstove full of smoldering ashes, then lay down, face tucked to paws, eyes cowering. The pungent smell of the dog's damp, filthy coat filled the shack.

Though Jenny and Moses had lived there for years, the shack seemed makeshift. Newspaper was tucked into the cracks in the walls, and a section of ribbing was exposed. There were two cots, a table, an illustrated Bible with a torn-out Bible page for a bookmark, and two crate chairs. A red tobacco tin, with a slit in its top, hung from the flue.

Jenny took the tin down and jangled it at her ear. I heard the coins. Her savings. "Take this to the bank, will you?" she said. "Get this much in five-cents. I never been in the bank. They don't know me."

With my pocketknife I pried open the tin, took out eight nickels, emptied the remaining money into a burlap bag I found in a corner, then went to the bank. I returned with $8.95 in nickels. Jenny sat at the table counting: "Five, five, five, five," and so on, without adding them up. Then she fit all but a few of the nickels back into the blue paper wrappers.

"I'll be at the jukebox now a lot," she said.

I sat down on a crate facing her. "Did you decide," I said, "who did this terrible thing to Moses?"

I should've run the errand and left her alone.

"Keep the nickels," she snapped, her face wrought up with anger. "Take them—damn, get out, you!" She pushed the nickels across the table. "God damn you, it's not your business now." She spit at my feet.

She sprawled across the table, looking as defeated as anyone I'd ever seen. Her head flat on the table, she talked sideways, to herself mostly. "Moses," she said, "was thirty-six. He didn't get married. Didn't give me a grandchild. Didn't even come home for supper that night. He was a good boy. He

would've got married. I can't figure why that man . . . don't
know what Moses did to that man to make him hate Moses.
Trap him that way. It's a shame. Look around this house,
there's food. Plenty of food. That's always here no matter
what. For Moses's supper." Then she sobbed, almost like she
was choking, and I left.

She quit her job, she began to drift between her shack and
the jukebox. I saw her cousins carrying food and scrap wood
to her shack.

Each morning as Jenny climbed the stairs to the loading
dock, I said hello, though there was never a reply. Sometimes
she seemed startled to hear a voice, to be addressed at all. As
the days passed, this came to seem like a normal arrangement.
Of course, when I think back on her allegiance to the jukebox,
it harbors a sad and disquieting reality. She might visit three
or four times a day.

She divvied up her nickels, one, maybe two for each visit,
all the while knowing the jukebox might be sent away at any
time. She'd be entranced as the disc fell and the music started.
"Moses, Moses," she'd chide. "That's not how I taught you
to sing."

Then, on December 28, the station seemed touched by a
premonitory chill. A storm had been forecast, and the life of
Churchill was quickened. Everyone hurried to stock up on
food. Storms came up so fast, they ambushed more than arrived. This storm proved no exception. All morning winds
careened off Hudson Bay, whistling shrilly, answered by howl-

ing dogs all over town. Snow piled up like levees along the riverbank, and in a matter of hours Churchill was locked in.

To me the morning felt odd; it was as if some natural line of descent from hour to hour had been jarred loose and was struggling to realign on its own. I was restless but at the same time didn't want to leave my office. To try and temper this, I sat down in front of Elias's game of solitaire, but my mind wandered and I gave up. I remained in my office, a fort against the weather; I sent my crew home. Shoulders hunched, faces wrapped in scarves, they set out like men entering the maw of the ice age. It was Thursday, so there was no train scheduled, but I had plenty of paperwork to do and enough food and coffee to hold me. I lay down on Elias's couch but couldn't get comfortable. The springs kept jabbing me.

I got up, stacked invoices, stoked up the fire, and checked the wood supply. Once everything was in order, I suddenly gave in to a year-long urge and tossed Elias's solitaire cards into the fire, cackling as if I'd been cooped up for a month already. I watched the cards blacken and shrivel. When I turned away, I saw Jenny's face in the door. The window had been frosted over, but she'd rubbed away a shape large enough for her eyes and nose. When her breath fogged the glass, she used her mitten to wipe it clean again. She wasn't wearing the mitten, but held it in her hand. It was minus 15 degrees out, I'd read that on the thermometer nailed just outside the door. That she was bare-handed shook me. I stood staring, waiting; her face sank away.

I went to the door, opened it a little, and struggled to keep it open against the wind. Though the jukebox was near the door, through the crack I had to more or less sight Jenny, much the way a bird would be viewed through binoculars; the world gives you just so much light, so much time. I watched Jenny reach to the bottom of the burlap bag, coming up with one nickel after another, which she slipped into the jukebox without pressing any buttons. The wind died down enough for me to hear Jenny say, "We'll have a nice, long talk, Moses. Would you like that?" She pressed buttons in rapid disorder, then slammed her fist down on them, then gently touched the jukebox. The smothering blizzard, the temperature dropping like an anvil. I closed the door and through a small, clear spot on the window watched her sit down, legs folded under her, mittens stuffed into her pockets. When the first song ended, she raised herself up enough to watch the next record drop, then sat down again. It then struck me that she'd measured out the remainder of her life.

As though swept in by the blizzard, Elias was suddenly on the dock. Spooked by Jenny's behavior, he'd stayed away for a while. I held the door open again and said, "Elias!" But he ignored me, or didn't hear me. Cursing, pulling at her collar, he tried to get Jenny to her feet. He worked frantically at this for a few minutes, then fell flat on his back, exhausted.

"Elias!" I shouted. "I'll help!" He looked at me then. Turning back to Jenny, he gave her a hard kick to the back, then started down the stairs. Stopping, he turned and looked directly at me, and said, "It's how she wants it."

My father told me once that the importance of any event was measured by your memory's loyalty to it. When he said that, he was facing away from me at his work table, painting on a wing stripe. He seemed to always say important things over his shoulder, as though seeing his face would make the wisdom too personal, as though it might not make true sense if I associated it with a human expression. To my father, words of wisdom might best be heard in the dark, or a whiteout.

The jukebox slowly was buried.

Before that day I hadn't given much thought to what might've become of Moses. Even if I'd known, I couldn't have convinced Jenny of it. The storm set up a kind of belligerent residency. No trains arrived; I found out later that the tracks north of Flin Flon were unpassable. The "flats" seemed a century's walk from the station. I set up house in the office, cooking meals, figuring the books. I burned the invoice; I'd see to it that Ruth Omik or Philomene Nuqac took the jukebox home.

I think about that time, often when I don't choose to; the memories just take over. Every few hours, I'd rubbed the window clean. I'd watched Jenny's decision enacted, actually saw her reach out a ghostly arm and let snow sculpt it to the jukebox, a bridge between her and her son. The blizzard continued for days after the jukebox was covered, after Jenny was. Well after I'd decided to leave Churchill.

Old Swimmers

LATE ON THE NIGHT OF JAKE'S FOURTEENTH BIRTHDAY, his mother said, "Helen drinks, you know, and lives by the ocean," but above the kitchen noise and through his bedroom door, Jake heard it as *Helen drinks from the ocean.* He took note of this eccentricity; he didn't believe it was true, only that it might be.

"God, not *again*," he muttered, sitting up in bed. "Idiots." He knew that his neighbors, the Anguilles, from two doors away on Franklin Street in Windsor were visiting, and that in their derisively spirited way everyone was maligning his aunt Helen. Helen lived alone in Halifax; Jake knew that much was true. His parents hadn't seen her in ten years. This summer, more sweltering than most, Peter and Belle Anguilles had dropped by almost every night. In his bedroom, Jake pictured the couple as he'd so often seen them: Peter, in his soiled undershirt that seemed to sweat on its own, shoes off, habitually nodding, agreeing with every indictment and rumor of Helen that Jake's parents set on the kitchen table like a red-flush poker hand. Belle, like her husband, was in her late forties. She wore heavy earrings that seemed responsible for her long face. Her gaze was intense; when bored, she'd turn it toward a window, blaming the world. Peter taught math in the same high school where Donald, Jake's father, taught wood shop. Belle and Alison, Jake's mother, wrote "verse" for the same greeting card company; Belle invented rhymed birthday wishes, while Alison dreamed up condolences—neither had bothered to give Jake a card at all.

Jake switched on the bedside lamp, took up his note pad and pen, and jotted two entries about the evening so far—later, he'd refer to his notes in his weekly letter to Helen. "They ate my birthday cake," he wrote. And: "My neighbors' name means 'eel'—I laugh whenever I think of that."

He placed the note pad and pen on his bed, then walked into the kitchen.

"Why, hello, Jakie," Belle Anguilles said.

Jake stared at the empty cake tin. With a low voice full of trembling and false hurt, he said, "Thanks—but no, I'll pass on the cake."

"Birthdays can wear you out," his father said. "It's midnight, or just about. Aren't you tired?"

110

Jake fit himself to the wall. He had on just his pajama bottoms. He was a wiry boy, with thick, neatly combed black hair and the faint shadow of a mustache, an aquiline nose, and dark brown eyes. In the presence of the Anguilles and his parents he was fidgety. He had a way of fixing a tight-lipped expression of distrust on his face, especially when someone he didn't like was talking. His face became a dare—Go ahead, try me. He did that now, in the kitchen, glaring at Belle Anguilles, making her uncomfortable enough to shift on her chair.

Jake's father shrugged, then carried on. "Helen," he said, "well—you must understand, her mind is unkempt. That *Caribou* ferry incident. She relives and relives it, poor thing. She's given her life to the past, and not a good past, either. And to those other old girls—what's their *club* called?"

"The WSCF," Jake's mother said promptly. "Stands for Women Survivors of the *Caribou* Ferry. It's all pitiable, really. They meet every summer, the women. Well, you could understand it for a few years after the war, couldn't you. A reunion and such. But it's gone on now, what . . . ?"

"Let's see," Jake's father said. "The ferry was sunk in 1942. So she's gone to *seventeen* reunions. Always at the Inn at Peggy's Cove. It's unnatural, is what I think, dwelling on the morbid that way. I mean, what can they find to talk about for an entire weekend—people drowning? It gives me the willies, truth be told. And of course she's never married, my dear

111

sister. Who'd want to have *that* for dinner conversation every night?"

The Anguilles looked incredulous, highly entertained.

Back in his room, the door closed, Jake opened his desk drawer and took out the issue of *Canadian History* that contained the article "The Sinking of the *Caribou* Ferry." He'd discovered it in a stack of free magazines at his neighborhood library. He sat on his bed and glanced through it, though he all but had it memorized. In October 1942, the *Caribou*, a vessel with nearly four hundred people aboard, was torpedoed and sunk by a German U-boat, the *Laughing Cow*. On that night of horror and confusion, the *Caribou* had been carrying U.S. and Canadian militia and Canadian citizens: 137 people were lost. This happened in a channel off Cape Breton Island, a town called Sydney. The tragedy was said to have brought the war to Canada. The article mentioned the annual WSCF reunion and included a photograph that Jake had scrutinized, but couldn't determine which survivor was his aunt. There were no photographs of Helen in his house.

One great quarrel, or a sequence of fallings-out—whatever, it had caused irreversible damage—had poisoned Jake's parents toward Helen. Jake wondered if it had happened in a year before he was born. When he was ten, he'd heard George and Alison complaining about Helen. He had his door open a crack. The sheer intensity of his parent's rancor had shocked him. Helen wasn't yet a presence in Jake's life, just a distant aunt he'd heard about but hadn't met. Soon, however, he realized that he wasn't being allowed to meet her. Over the following months, he learned to recognize the peculiar pitch of his parent's voices, the indelicate details as being about his aunt, and he eavesdropped on dozens of their conversations. He grew more and more ashamed of them, convinced that they invented aberrations and misfortunes, assigned them to Helen, then fully subscribed to them as truths. As a result of one of those mysterious, lopsided balances of the heart that such profound shame can engender, Jake began to feel *connected* to Helen, as he became further estranged from his parents. Helen was his parents' preoccupation, and Jake's, too. She was their fallen world—they aimed dissatisfactions with their own life at Helen. So did Jake confide his own week's activities, moods, assessments of life, even dreams to her—in his letters.

Now, having latched on to the notion that his aunt perhaps ladled seawater into her mouth, he decided to begin his letter:

> *Dear Aunt Helen,*
> *If you don't wish to discuss why you drink from the ocean, I won't push it.*

There had been hundreds of letters over a four-year period. Each was essentially an act of ironic persistence, simply because Jake had never received a reply. Not a single postcard. He'd never seen *Halifax* stamped on an envelope. Helen had

113

gotten the letters; none had been returned. Jake knew her address: 406 Robie Street. He'd called the Halifax operator from a pay phone, and she'd told him. His letters to Helen were sometimes thirty or forty pages in length. He was passionately dedicated to them, if not yet to his aunt.

Then, several weeks after his birthday, a postcard arrived. In cramped handwriting, with no salutation or signature, it read: "Nephew, you have worn me down. Why not visit." Though less than cheered by its negative tone, the very presence of the postcard, with its picture of the Historic Properties section of Halifax—a few cobblestone buildings, outdoor tables, tourists—felt like a victory. His heart virtually leapt at the opportunity to visit The Maritimes. That evening, when he approached his parents, that's precisely how he put it. "I'd like to visit The Maritimes," he said, attempting to camouflage Helen's irksome existence within the entire foggy coast of eastern Canada. George and Alison were at the kitchen table, reading different sections of the paper. "We don't have to yell a lot," Jake said. "Don't say no—I'm going." He handed his mother Helen's postcard.

One o'clock the next morning, Jake sat at his desk composing a letter. He described the previous day's weather, then went on at length about studying the Nova Scotia section of the encyclopedia, leading up to this:

> *Oh, by the way, I'm coming to visit. I showed Mom*
> *and Dad your postcard. I said that I was going. We*

argued all night. It was awful. Finally, they gave in.
They said you'd have to send a card directly to them. You
have to say that you want me to visit.

Your nephew,
Jake

The letter filled twenty-eight note pages and ended with
a P.S.: "I want you to know that I've forgiven you for not
answering my letters for four years. You must be awfully
busy."

He couldn't sleep. He began rehearsing ways to greet Helen. He even struck a few poses, first throwing his head back,
assuming a serious expression, his hands continually engaged
in one outlandish gesture or another. "Why, hello, Helen.
How kind of you to invite me."

A week after posting his letter, Jake's parents received a
card: "Jake is invited." The next day, having specially come
home for her lunch hour, Alison phoned her sister-in-law,
grimacing at the mouthpiece as if at Helen's remembered
face. After making arrangements for Jake's arrival, Alison said,
"One last thing, Helen. Jake is allergic even to rubbing al-
cohol. A whiff of Scotch, he swells up like a balloon." Having
thus lied, Alison hung up.

The following Saturday morning before dawn, after a hurried breakfast, Jake's father drove him to the train station.

Yawning, Donald said, "Your mother thinks this trip of yours is unhealthy. But try to enjoy yourself."

Jake thought he sensed a conciliatory mood. He wanted to ask for five more dollars, and to reach out and shake his father's hand, but decided against both. His father stopped the car at the curb in front of the station. The entrance lights were pale in the first daylight. Two redcap attendants stood behind the wide glass doors, drinking coffee. "Got your money?" Donald said. It was clear that he wasn't going to escort Jake to the ticket booth or see him to the train.

Jake said, "Yeah, thanks for the loan. See you." He stepped from the car, took up his suitcase, and walked into the station.

The train left Windsor at 6:05. Inspecting all six passenger cars, Jake finally settled onto a seat in a car occupied by one elderly man who was snoring, and had a scarf wrapped around his neck even though the car wasn't air-conditioned. Jake took his pen and note pad from the zippered compartment, then hoisted his suitcase onto the luggage rack. Sitting down, he began a letter to Helen, first describing the train station.

An hour's drive from Halifax, Peggy's Cove was a popular tourist spot. Yet half a mile along the jigsaw coastline, past the lighthouse that dominated the peninsula, Helen found some privacy. There the beach of gray stones met the cliffs, waves roughhoused moored dinghies, signs warned of undertows. Even young swimmers, Helen thought, wouldn't hazard this stretch of the ocean. "Ankle-deep," she recalled Thomas Pearcy saying. "A truly strong undertow can trip you up, even if you're standing ankle-deep." Helen was sixty-eight. Thomas, seventy-one, was her fiancé. Along her walk back to the inn, she was thinking of how they'd met. "I'll get my memories right up to the present," she said. Her feet were already achy. Later, she thought, I'll soak them in the tub. She took in the view. The sea was a lighter gray than the stones. Occasionally, small fish leapt and spun from the surface, disappearing without a splash. There were a few scraggly trees growing at odd angles right out of the cliffside. "Yes," she said, "I'll confirm my memories of Thomas, so that I'll be all caught up on them by the time we're married tomorrow."

Two years before, she and Thomas had met in the Ketch Harbor Post Office. That morning, Thomas said, "I believe I saw you here around this time last year."

"What a good memory you have," Helen said.

He invited her to sit on a bench outside. It was a Thursday. In the course of their rather disconnected conversation, Thomas mentioned that he was a retired naval officer, and that he'd moved to Ketch Harbor to be near his nephew's family. Helen asked which years he'd served.

"From 1930 to 1948," he said. "Yes, but after the *Caribou* ferry sank, I was in hospital for six weeks, pneumonia and broken ribs, and I'm afraid I never went to sea again."

Quite astounded, Helen all but cried out, "You were there?"

"Second officer," Thomas said.

Thomas was the first man to whom Helen recounted her own experiences on the *Caribou*. She spoke slowly and in detail, and when she was finished, Thomas said that he'd heard of the WSCF and in fact envied the women and found their reunions painfully courageous. "Yes," he said. "I keep so much to myself. I still have nightmares. They can't be helped. Certain faces come at me." He looked at the sidewalk.

"Only if you'd like," Helen said. "We can perhaps talk another time."

"Such as Harold Tavernor," Thomas said. "A friend if there ever was one. He was the wireless operator. That night, I was in the wireless room with Harold. He said, 'I've got an uneasy mind about something.' Those were the exact words he said. Then the explosion, and when the *Caribou* listed over, suddenly we had water up to our knees. We heard water pouring into the other compartments. Harold was frantically trying the wireless, but it was all static. We heard shouting."

"You might've heard me," Helen said. "Because I wasn't brave and going about something useful. I saw fire and I shouted, though I can't recall what."

"Then the ceiling broke open," Thomas said. "It fell down on us. Then we found ourselves outside. I say that, but I don't remember how we got there, if we pushed the door open or the water did that for us. On deck Harold put his hands in his pockets, just like he was standing on a street corner, talking."

"I was fortunate," Helen said. "I got on a lifeboat right away."

"Then the ferry tilted," Thomas said.

"Yes," Helen said, "right out of the water."

"Nobody left on board could afford to wait any longer," Thomas said.

"They had to jump," Helen said.

"I jumped," Thomas said. "The water was cold, but I didn't mind. Maybe it was the shock. A lifeboat passed me by. I tried to get on it, and somebody called out that it was too crowded. I got on another one, a wooden raft with oil drums for floats."

"We didn't say much or sing hymns," Helen said. "But we heard hymns in the dark."

"On ours we had hymns," Thomas said.

"Every raft was different," Helen said. "My friends agree on that."

"So many people floated away in their life belts," Thomas said. "I saw a woman, or a girl, floating dead the next morning. And if she'd just come out of the beauty parlor, her hair couldn't have been any better."

"That's a hard sight," Helen said. "And Harold?"

"I felt right away Harold was lost," Thomas said.

After a few moments of silence, Helen said, "I must be getting back to the inn."

Helen wrote down her phone number in Halifax on a piece of paper.

"Thank you," Thomas said, surprised, "I'd appreciate it if we spoke with one another before next summer."

Thomas phoned Helen every Wednesday for six months and visited every weekend after that; then, he proposed marriage. After three weeks of thinking it over, Helen accepted, stipulating that the ceremony take place at the inn during the WSCF reunion. "It's not that I need the other's approval," she assured Thomas. "But I'd be happier for it."

Helen's feet were throbbing by the time she reached the inn. Sitting on the front steps, she rubbed them and looked at the swimmers, her friends. Though it was 1959, they wore swim outfits that were popular in the 1930s: flared cotton shorts and floral-pattern chintz skirts, with loosely drawn tops whose necklines veered just low enough to reveal a seductive modesty—whether this was vanity or nostalgia was difficult to know, since the youngest woman in the ocean was over sixty. A few stood in the shallows, cupping water over themselves. Some managed the breaststroke for short distances. Others waded well back from the warning buoy: NO SWIMMERS BEYOND THIS POINT.

Helen thought about the uncanny powers of recall the WSCF had, or perhaps at the reunion they allowed themselves certain details too painful to bear alone. Take suitcases, the spontaneous subject at that morning's breakfast table. Of all things! Suitcases floating near the rafts. A remarkable array of anecdotes, told one by one, as coffee was sipped and heads nodded, *Yes, that's how it was.* Which suitcases were heirlooms and which had been purchased in shops. Suitcase linings were discussed; their ruffled, silk pockets. Memories so fully steeped in loss that they couldn't be sentimental. More, they were like tangible objects drawn forth with weight and presence, as though the breakfast conversation was unwittingly a séance. As Helen looked at the brightly colored towels along the beach, the shawls, the sun hats, it seemed for a moment that the lost suitcases that had been floating in the sea for almost twenty years had washed ashore and burst open.

Helen walked across the wide porch, then through the hallway and up the stairs to her room. She soaked her feet in the tub for half an hour. She dressed in slacks, a light green blouse, a shawl, white flats, then looked in the closet at her wedding dress. It had been her grandmother's; it was intricately embroidered, with a lace collar and hem. Helen walked down the stairs and out to the parking lot. Many of her friends were making their way up from the beach. She got into her Buick sedan and drove to Halifax to pick up her nephew.

Jake was the only person in the cavernous terminal who appeared lost. He stood away from any bench, staring at the front doors, holding his suitcase. He had on a light brown jacket torn at one cuff, over a white short-sleeve shirt, blue jeans, socks, and tennis shoes. He had a slightly worried expression.

At the entrance, Helen fumbled in her pocketbook, found a cigarette, lighted it, took a few deep draws, then extinguished it in a standing metal ashtray. "My pen pal," she said to herself, then walked up to Jake.

"Jake?" she said.

They didn't hug; Jake still held his suitcase. They shook hands.

"Not much family resemblance between us, is there?" he said. He handed Helen a thick envelope containing the letter he'd written on the train.

"Why, Jake," Helen said. "There's stamps on this envelope."

"In case you didn't show up," Jake said. "I'd of mailed it."

The schedule board, high on a wall, loudly clicked in arrival and departure times and track numbers. They both looked at it.

"Want me to leave?" Jake said. "Maybe this is a bad idea."

Helen took a hard look at Jake's face, but said nothing. She turned and walked toward the front doors. Jake followed her to the car, then sat in the roomy backseat next to his suitcase.

Driving slowly down Barrington Street, Helen asked, "Why do you write me so many letters, Jake? This new one in my purse is nearly as long as the Holy Book." She glanced at Jake in the rearview mirror.

"The letters should've explained that," Jake said.

"Well, you have a rare life that's more than imagination," Helen said. "It's *that* rough at home."

"Maybe worse than I wrote you," Jake said.

They drove through a warehouse district, then turned off onto a main street that ran along Citadel Park. "Want to see my house?" Helen said.

"Aren't we going to it?" Jake said.

"We're on Robie," Helen said, slowing down the car. "And that's my house."

She pointed to a one-story house, white with black shutters and a storm porch, peeling eaves, and a flower garden that looked cared for though not manicured.

They drove on past.

"Maybe we'll come back in a few days," Helen said.

"What about tonight?" Jake said.

"I've got to speak with you about something," Helen said. "I know we've just met. But the thing is, *tonight*—tonight we're staying at an inn, out by the ocean. Sounds nice, doesn't it? You'll like it, Jake. There's some people there I'd like you to meet."

"I'm not sure I like meeting just you yet," Jake said.

"Believe me," Helen said, "I understand. It's all so new and strange, isn't it? Jake, you don't have to like me, you know. You only have to not dislike me as much as you seem to dislike your mother and father. That way, you'll have adults to compare."

"Who are these people I'm going to like so much?" Jake said.

"Some friends of mine," Helen said. "And—"

Helen saw Jake staring into the rearview mirror.

"And," she said, "my fiancé."

"You're getting *married?*" Jake said. He pressed his head to the front seat.

"I'm sixty-eight," Helen said. "Do you suppose that's old enough?"

"*When* are you getting married?" Jake said.

"Let's put it this way," Helen said, "the postcard I sent you was a wedding invitation."

"That postcard didn't have the word *wedding* on it," Jake said.

Helen stopped the car alongside the curb and put it in neutral. She turned and looked at Jake. "I wanted a relative at my wedding," she said. "That's a natural thing to want. You're the only relative I can stand, and maybe that's because we hadn't met. Thomas, he's my fiancé. He's not a relative yet, technically speaking. I can turn the car around and go right back to the train. If you want that, say so. Otherwise, you can be my one relative at my wedding."

"Some visit," Jake said.

"You can mail me your impressions later," Helen said.

They drove out of Halifax, past the first small fishing village. Jake turned to look back at the pastel houses near the water; near one house was a lime-colored barn. It was like this all along the coast, bright yellow, blue, pink matchbox houses, some on stilts among the boulders. The lobster boats and trawlers were painted in identical hues.

"People my age do get married, you know," Helen said.

"I figured that out already," Jake said.

"My friend Elizabeth, who's seventy. She married recently." Helen said. "She had her reasons."

"What were they?" Jake said.

"They were hers," Helen said. "I didn't ask."

"I guess I'm not supposed to ask, either," Jake said.

"You may ask," Helen said.

"Why are you getting married?" Jake said.

"Because," Helen said, then weighed out her words carefully. "Thomas, my fiancé, chooses to remember the same things I do."

They arrived at the Inn at Peggy's Cove. It was dusk. Carrying his suitcase onto the porch, Jake looked through the enormous windows into the dining room. Waiters held three or four wineglasses in each hand like jugglers; they were setting the long table.

On the porch Helen introduced Jake to several women. They each wore a name tag pinned to their blouse or sweater. Under the name were the initials "NS" or "NB" or "NF," which Jake figured right away stood for the Maritime Provinces, Nova Scotia, New Brunswick, and Newfoundland.

Helen showed Jake upstairs to his room. "Wash up, change clothes if you'd like. I'd suggest that," she said. "Then come down for dinner."

"Who are those women?" Jake said.

"My maids of honor," Helen said. "Just wash up."

Like glass jellyfish, chandeliers lit the dining room. Jake had put on his dress trousers and a new shirt, but still wore his jacket as well. From the stairs he counted five waiters in attendance. They poured wine, lit candles, refilled water glasses, all in an air of subdued celebration. Then Jake counted the guests: twenty-six women. Starting toward an empty chair at the table, he detoured through the swinging door into the kitchen. Away from the ovens, he watched two cooks at work. The kitchen was alive with chatter, in French and English, and there was a steady traffic of waiters in and out of the door.

One cook, a tall, robust man wearing a French chef's hat and apron, cast an annoyed look at Jake. "Who are you?" he said.

"I'm here with my aunt," Jake said. "Her name's Helen. Let me ask you, who are those other women?"

"She didn't tell you?" the cook said.

"I know she's getting married," Jake said.

On a table to his immediate left Jake saw a three-tiered wedding cake. There was a plastic bride and groom in a cellophane wrapper next to the cake.

"I made that," the cook said. "Frosting will be added to-morrow. I'll write the names on it. It'll be ready by noon."

"Is that when the wedding is?" Jake said.

"Your aunt Helen keeps a lot of secrets, doesn't she?" the cook said.

"Do you know for sure who those women are?" Jake said.

"The ones who didn't drown on the *Caribou* ferry," he said. "It's a famous reunion, at least in Ketch Harbor."

"I thought so," Jake said. "I thought it was them."

"They're here every summer," the cook said, "but this is the first cake I've made for any of them. Now, son, it is best that you leave us alone to our work here."

Jake walked back into the dining room and found Helen. "I know who these women are," he said.

"Who told you?" she said. "Jake, I would've told you, eventually."

"I saw their picture in a magazine," Jake said. "You were with them, too."

Helen looked over and saw Thomas Pearcy near the front door. "Excuse me, Jake," she said, then walked over to Thomas and kissed him on the cheek. Arm in arm, they walked to the table and sat next to each other. Jake sat on a chair directly across from the couple. He took in Thomas's calm, weathered face, gray hair, still-black eyebrows. Even while sitting he appeared tall. He was deliberate in his gestures. Jake met his glance twice. Both times he half smiled, then looked away at nothing in particular. Jake wondered if his aunt had mentioned him to Thomas.

Jake noticed intermittent crescendos of talk; he realized the rise or fall in volume depended on which of the women was most hard of hearing and which had to raise her voice. His field of vision was suddenly obscured when the women on either side leaned over and consulted with each other on the subject of Helen's near marriage to a tailor in Halifax.

"Why didn't she marry him?" Jake said.

Close to his face, both women stared at him. Then one whose tag read Eleanor Bates, NS, said, "Because, my dear, he was a good tailor but not good company, with no outstanding memories to speak of. It would have been a mistake, done out of loneliness. And Helen has mostly enjoyed her solitude. Besides, Helen's done well for herself with Mr. Pearcy, and he with her."

All through the servings of cucumber soup, plates of salmon with asparagus, there was the constant murmur of conversation. Thomas and Helen said barely two words to each other.

When the table was cleared and dessert plates and coffee cups brought out, Mrs. J. Prosper, NB, who sat next to Jake, beckoned the headwaiter. He leaned over, and Mrs. Prosper requested that he and the other waiters keep to the kitchen until called for. She said this with such unblinking authority that there was no room for debate. The waiters disappeared.

Then, Mrs. Prosper tapped her water glass with her spoon, a call to order.

When the table quieted down, Mrs. Prosper said, "Mr. Pearcy—welcome. Helen has spoken of you often and quite highly. And in no uncertain terms. We understand you served as second officer on . . ."

Thomas stood up, in effect interrupting Mrs. Prosper. Helen stared at her plate. After a moment, Thomas said, "Helen told me that she preferred for us to meet before the wedding. So, please, take a good look. I was on the ferry. I'm part of your recollections, whether you saw me on that voyage or not. As far as Helen and I are concerned, I can say, for myself, that we're marrying for love and similar moments in our past, and for other reasons that are nobody's business."

Thomas waited for somebody to speak. Adele Heaney, NS, gathered herself to her feet. Both hands on the table, she said, "I saw a dark shadow before it submerged again. I'd handed two babies down to a raft. When I looked up, I saw it. What else could it have been but the *Laughing Cow?*"

She paused, then drank some water. "The truth is, Mr. Pearcy, some died in the water and some died inside because they lost—well, I lost every cousin I had."

Adele Heaney sat down.

Silence drifted into the room like a change of weather. Helen traced her finger along the table edge. Thomas drank his entire glass of wine, then sat down. Jake got up from the table and walked back into the kitchen; he found the cooks and waiters playing cards. A waiter looked at Jake, then back to his bid. Jake went to the counter, took up the platter of sliced honey cake, and carried it out into the dining room. Beginning with Helen, he served dessert, though many women refused. It was late; the ocean breeze was picking up. A gust occasionally fluted the porch. Some of the women put on shawls. Others drifted upstairs. Abruptly, as though hypnotized, a few fell asleep, heads tilted back, mouths open— or having closed their eyes while sitting upright. With folded napkins or sweaters as pillows, others slept heads down on the table. Thomas fell asleep, head on hands. Helen drank the untouched glass of wine on her left.

Jake sat on the stairs looking at the table of sleeping women. He then walked to Helen's chair, helped her to her feet, and guided her upstairs. "I should have coffee," she said. "The sun all day, now the wine." Her legs were wobbly. "It's 205," she instructed Jake. The door was open. Helen lay down on the bed.

"Why did only one woman tell her story?" Jake said.

"There's a proverb," Helen said. "To taste the sea, all you need is one gulp."

By the time Jake removed her shoes and covered her with a quilt, Helen was asleep. He draped a blanket over the east-facing window so the sun wouldn't strike her eyes in the morning. Out in the hallway, Jake remembered Helen's eyeglasses. He returned to her bedside, removed them from her face, and before placing them on the dresser tried them on. He could barely make out the objects in the room.

Downstairs, Jake switched off the chandeliers. He heard the cooks and waiters getting rowdy, shouting numbers. Moonlight illuminated the porch. Jostling him awake, Jake slung Thomas Pearcy's arm over his own shoulder, then, stopping on each stair, maneuvered him down the hall. Jake found Thomas's room key in his suit coat pocket. In his room, Thomas sprawled on the bed. Jake helped him out of his suit coat, took off his shoes, and covered him with a blanket.

That was how they were introduced.

Jake went back downstairs and sat on the porch. He still felt the movement of the train. He knew that he'd be awake all night. Maybe in a while, he thought, he'd be of some use. He'd go back upstairs, get Helen's wedding dress, and walk with it on the beach. He'd let the wind fill it like a sail. It would be fresh with sea air for the wedding. Jake had noticed the dress in Helen's closet.

Laughing and Crying

KEDRICK WATCHED HIS MOTHER, DAHLIA, RUMMAGE through the kitchen drawers for sparklers. Come September, he'd be in the eighth grade. He was spindly, sandy-haired, not too athletic. But he had an old-fashioned mechanical sensibility, which he'd discovered on his own. He belonged to the school's radio club and could repair a radio without using a manual. His father, Dalton, was a conductor on the B&O local. He lived in Lapaz, Indiana, ten minutes by rail from Mishawaka. Dalton and Dahlia had been divorced a year.

"I'm going to forgive you," Dahlia said, "it being Independence Day, though it's not officially a forgiving type of holiday. I'm angry, that I'll admit. But I won't say another word about last night, though I know you were at that godforsaken three-D movie with that friend of your father's."

She was thirty-six, lanky, with beautiful skin and almond-brown eyes. She had a recent nervous habit of raking her fingers through her hair, letting it fall in bangs across her forehead. She'd tweezed out her gray hairs.

"It was a good movie," Kedrick said. "Space monsters invaded and President Eisenhower sent in the army. There's a happy ending, Mom. What do you want?"

"I want you to get that three-D movie out of your head," Dahlia said. "It's not good having any kind of movie in your head, but especially that kind. And I *don't* want you at the Savoy tonight. We're picketing out front. I want you home. You might have noticed I've already been to visit the bottle this morning. You know how jittery I get during tornado season. I've got so much on my mind. There's an afternoon of watching the McCarthy hearings, and a night of weather reports ahead of me."

In the basement was a five-by-seven shelter.

Dahlia finally located the sparklers in a drawer next to the sink. "It's still drizzling outside," she said. "We'll have to wave these right here in the kitchen."

She stuck half a dozen sparklers into a piece of stale coffee cake and lit them. They fizzled and popped, shooting sparks and filling the kitchen with an acrid smell that made Kedrick cough and snort like a bull. She then lit two more sparklers and hopped and spun around, making flower shapes in the air with them. "Independence Day!" she sang. "Come on, honey.

Don't be a grump. We've got the house. We've got each other. There's a lot to celebrate!" she said in an almost self-acusing tone. This put Kedrick on edge. "Grumpy, grumpy, grumpy," Dahlia said. She dipped and floated around the kitchen like an oversize marionette, arms and legs out of control, cackling, taunting her son.

When he'd had enough, Kedrick shouted, "Thought you said you forgave me!" He ran to his bedroom, slammed the door, and turned the lock.

Laughing and crying, Dahlia followed him. Through the door, Kedrick could hear the sparklers. "Honey," she said, "I'm sorry. I really am. Come on out. I'm sorry. It's just this crazy weather. You know tornado weather makes me a little fruity."

Kedrick got under the sheet and pushed his face into his pillow. "Kedrick," his mother said, "I know you've got the pillow over your head." After a few minutes, she went back to the kitchen. He could hear her tossing the charred sparkler wicks into the trash. He looked at his desk clock; it was 11:30, time to watch his father.

He took up his binoculars, jimmied loose the screen window, and slipped out into the backyard. He crossed two neighbors' yards, then walked three blocks to the schoolyard. At 11:45, Audubon Spivey, his father's best friend, drove his Studebaker over the curb at the intersection of Woodlawn and Ash, half a block from the school. He parked on a gravel patch beside the warning X. Through the binoculars, Kedrick saw that Audubon wore a baseball cap and nodded an unlit cigarette between his lips. Precisely at noon the train arrived, screeching to a stop. The caboose was just yards from the intersection. Kedrick's father appeared behind the trellis gate of the caboose. Over his uniform he wore a black rain slicker. Audubon got out of his car and walked over. He handed Dalton up a sandwich wrapped in aluminum foil, an apple, and a paper cup of coffee. Kedrick knew it was coffee; that was all he'd ever seen his father drink. Then Audubon unwrapped his own sandwich. He couldn't climb aboard. It was against regulations.

Kedrick watched them eat and talk. At one point, Dalton punched the air, grimacing. What was that about? Kedrick wondered. At 12:21, the train rumbled off. Audubon got back in the Studebaker, and Kedrick walked home.

Audubon was a bachelor. He and Dalton were born in Mishawaka and had been childhood pals. They'd served in the army together, and when they got home, Dalton married Dahlia and Audubon brought the flagging Savoy back to life. Kedrick knew that Audubon and Dalton had lunch together every weekday. If he wanted information about his father, he went to the Savoy, sat in Audubon's office, and asked. Audubon never refused, though he'd often weigh a fact a long time before offering it. Audubon never felt that his loyalty to Dalton was being tested, just that a new loyalty to Kedrick had begun. One afternoon, Kedrick sat on the leather swivel chair across from Audubon's desk, watching him toss crumbled mimeographs of "Coming Attractions" at the fan, which ricocheted them all over the room. "Kedrick," he said, "your father is lonely in the worst way. He wants there to be a good world out there, but he wants nothing to do with it. He likes being a conductor. He likes living alone. Even with me—me, who he's known forever, he can still close up like a root cellar. Basically, he keeps his distance from every single minute. He's what they call aloof. That drove Dahlia up a wall."

Just last week, Kedrick learned that Dalton was living in half a duplex on Harland Street. He'd been dating a telephone operator named Evelyn, who, according to Audubon, looked "like an older Frances Farmer, the beautiful but tormented actress." Also, Dalton's living room was furnished exactly like the one in his former house on Ash. It had the same type of draperies, chairs, couch, floor radio, pleated hassock.

The night before, Audubon had given Kedrick a private screening of *They Came to Earth*, the science-fiction movie he'd ordered along with a hundred pair of 3-D glasses for a trial week. This was opening night, and Kedrick promised he'd be there, no matter what. He'd been following the progress of 3-D in the country, mainly through Chicago radio and newspapers he'd read in the library. Over his bed, he'd tacked up a postcard of a packed audience at the Taft movie house in Chicago. Hundreds of devotees in 3-D glasses leaned forward as if mesmerized.

When he got home from the train, Dahlia was in the living room watching the hearings. The television was next to the radio. Looking in, Kedrick saw that Dahlia was nailing together her placard for the demonstration. In bold lettering across the top it read 3-D DISTORTS REALITY, and along the bottom were the words COMMUNIST PLOT.

At 5:30, Kedrick wandered into the kitchen. Dahlia slid out two TV dinners. "Beef or chicken?" she said.

"I can't tell any difference with those," Kedrick said.

Dahlia shrugged. "Fine," she said. She sat opposite Kedrick at the table, took up her knife, and meticulous as a surgeon cut into the aluminum cover of one tray. A thick steam rushed out. She inhaled it deeply. "Guess I'll have the chicken," she said. She slid the other plate to Kedrick. She then carried her tray to the living room, sat down on a chair in front of the radio, and began to eat her mashed potatoes from their compartment.

All through supper, Dahlia fussed with the dial, listening to weathermen. The brown, oval-topped Philco was over three feet high with a black screen and black dials. Some years back Dahlia had scratched the names of the cities she could reach above their frequencies: Terre Haute, Indianapolis, Chicago, Cincinnati, Des Moines, even cities in states as far away as Missouri, Kansas, Oklahoma. Turning the dial, she cast a wide ear over tornado country.

"Terre Haute weather says a tornado alert is in effect until nine P.M., Dahlia called in to the kitchen.

"That's not a *warning*, though," Kedrick said loudly.

"An alert," Dahlia said, turning down the volume, "generally means to keep glued to the radio until a warning comes on."

"Maybe you should take the transistor radio with you to your picketing tonight, Mom," Kedrick said. "Audubon's got a basement there he'd let you into."

"I don't appreciate your tone, young man," Dahlia said. She turned up the radio.

The day had been a scorcher. Now, at 7:30, it was still a stifling 85 degrees. From his Studebaker, Audubon watched the boycotters march in a wavering, oblong formation, each placard looking as if it weighed a ton. Audubon got out and shouted, "Crucify me, you bastards! After all the fun nights I gave you!" Tall, gaunt, with an unkempt shock of red hair, he looked like a scarecrow in the heat. He leaned. Even in the brief distance from the curb to the Savoy, it looked as if he were being yanked forward by an invisible rope attached to his chest. Grudgingly, the boycotters gave way.

Inside, Audubon unlocked the alley door, opened it, and there stood Kedrick. They both walked to the lobby. "Have a Mars bar on the house," Audubon said. "It's just you and me got the run of the place."

Kedrick went behind the counter and tucked a Mars bar in his shirt pocket. Then he looked at the front door, whose shades were rolled up just enough to see the boycotters' feet. "There's my mother's shoes," he said. "Yep, those blue sneakers are hers all right."

"Too bad," Audubon said, starting up the stairs. "They could be having a nice air-conditioned evening in here watching a movie, instead of sweating into their lemonade. Bitching about God and three-D and the like. You ask me, the heat's got people haywire. Hey, what say afterward we go to Middleton's, a root beer?"

"Good deal," Kedrick said.

The box of 3-D glasses were at the aisle door. Kedrick reached in as though picking a raffle winner and took up a white-rimmed pair. After showing himself to a center seat, he put on the glasses. Turning, he looked up at the brightly lit window of the projection booth. "Okay!" he shouted. "Ready!"

Audubon dimmed the theater lights and started up the projector. Downstairs, he got his own pair of glasses and sat in the back row.

Eighty minutes later, Kedrick applauded alone. He met Audubon in the lobby. Putting the 3-D glasses in the pocket where the Mars bar had been, he said, "That was great. Better the second time."

"Let's get over to Middleton's," Audubon said. "Closes in half an hour."

"People still out front?" Kedrick said.

"Yes, sir," Audubon said.

Leaving by the alley door, they went around behind the Savoy and over to Middleton's Pharmacy on the next block. "Sneaking through the town I was born in's disgusting," Audubon said. They sat at the counter, shirts soaked with sweat. Donny Middleton, Kedrick's schoolmate and the pharmacist's son, was on duty. He was a roly-poly, freckled boy who wore an oval paper hat and a white apron. "Two root beers," Audubon said. Donny drew the foam from a helmet-headed spigot and set the glasses on the counter. Audubon pressed the beading glass to his forehead.

"Put these on my tab," Audubon said.

"My dad said no more of that in your case," Donny said.

"Soda *jerk*," Kedrick said.

Donny got up close to Kedrick's face. "What's it like," he said. "Movie jump out at you, or what? I heard that three-D jumps right at you."

"Back off, Donny," Kedrick said, "I'll brain you."

Donny went to the far end of the counter and sponged an already clean section.

Audubon slurped down the last of his root beer. Kedrick took his slowly. Adjusting his 3-D glasses over his ears, he looked over at Donny. "Donny," he said, "I ever tell you that you're the only person I ever knew gets bigger when you take off your coat?"

"Commie rat," Donny said.

"Stop that cruelty," Audubon said, laughing a little. "Donny can't help he's fat."

"Yes he can," Kedrick said. "Why do you think he works here next to the ice cream, the soda jerk. No customer around for five minutes, he's at the chocolates."

"Three-D commie rat!" Donny piped up.

"God," Audubon sighed, "it's like a plague."

"You know something?" Kedrick said to Donny. "With these glasses on, looking at you? It's not three-D, it's *four*-D."

"Real funny," Donny said.

"How about a lift home?" Audubon said, leaving change on the counter.

"Nix," Kedrick said. "Mom's gonna be hopping mad I'm out. She'll know where I've been. That's what I've got waiting, so why should I hurry?"

"I'm going over to see Dalton tomorrow after supper," Audubon said. "Are you interested?'

"Divorce law says he's supposed to visit us at home," Kedrick said.

"Have you seen him at your house in a year?" Audubon said.

"No," Kedrick said.

"Try to work it out with your mother," Audubon said. "It's a good idea, you and Dalton talk. Maybe it's too bad you have to take the first step, but hell's bells, somebody has to."

"I'll be near the tracks, corner of Woodlawn and Ash. What time?" Kedrick said.

"How about six-thirty?" Audubon said.

. . .

The radio woke Kedrick. He'd slept late. He got out of bed and walked into the kitchen. The screen door was open and Dahlia was on the porch, staring at the horizon, where a rumbling charcoal squall was haloed in crab-apple light.

"Good morning, Mother," Kedrick said.

Dahlia turned sharply. "Only a dumb onion would risk more than a quick walk outside today," she said. "I've had my breakfast. The alimony was in the mail, but I won't go to the bank until tomorrow with it. So far six weather reports agree, a tornado will sweep through this afternoon or early this evening, and there's little chance it won't. So at three o'clock, I'll be in the shelter and you should be, too, Kedrick."

They ate separate lunches, and promptly at three, Dahlia carried a box full of sandwiches, a thermos of bourbon, and a flashlight down to the shelter. She already had a chair and hassock there. Kedrick watched from the kitchen doorway. "It's clearing up out there," he said. "Take a look."

"That peace and quiet crap's a tornado's best trick," Dahlia snapped. "I've got the transistor in this box. You can listen to the Philco, if you're so determined to run down the stairs at the last second."

Soon Kedrick heard Dahlia tune in to her favorite station, which played selections from the thirties and forties; she sang along loudly to "Across the Alley from the Alamo." Kedrick knew that she'd opened the thermos.

Kedrick ate a bologna sandwich, then worked on a new radio kit; around 5:30, he went to the basement and found Dahlia asleep on her chair. The empty thermos was on the floor. He switched off the radio, then took the flashlight from its box and put it on Dahlia's lap.

Carrying his rain parka, he walked to the warning X. The air was thick and muggy, and Kedrick heard the whirr of bark beetles. In a few minutes, Audubon drove up and Kedrick got in the front seat. Audubon wore blue work trousers and a T-shirt. Posters for *They Came to Earth* were in back.

As they started toward the interstate, Kedrick said, "You're keeping the Savoy closed tonight, aren't you."

"Useless not to," Audubon said. "Boycotters were there by five. They had their leftover sparklers and protest signs. Your mother didn't show up, though."

"Trying three-D was a brave thing," Kedrick said. "You're a hero, Audubon."

"Makes me want to laugh and cry both," he said. "Thirteen years in the movie business, all leads up to a stupid mistake."

"People abandoned you," Kedrick said. "I'd take it real personal if I was you."

"I just might hold a grudge," Audubon said.

"But the Savoy," Kedrick said. "You told me yourself it was already in deep trouble."

"Deeper than that," Audubon said. "I just tried to give three-D a home for a week. That was my intention, but people made it like breaking one of the Commandments. For Mishawaka, three-D was a piss-poor idea. Drew the wrath. Who could've guessed?"

They reached the outskirts of Lapaz, which was mostly outskirts; there was a cluster of streets immediately surrounded by farmland. They passed a grassy square with a fountain and a World War II tank netted with rust. On two sides of the square were shops; on the other two, residential streets. There were Colonial houses, mostly, and a few duplexes.

Audubon glanced at Kedrick, then back to his driving. "Dalton's been laid off," he said. They turned on to Harland Street. "Some sort of seniority deal. Switchmen, brakemen, conductors, all were let go. This is a bad hand he's been dealt. You lose a job it's a merciless thing. Especially on a holiday."

"What'll he do?" Kedrick said.

"I can't say what else he's cut out for, other than conductoring," Audubon said. "Now I'm going to give him my news, that the Savoy's gone under."

"I've got nothing at all to tell him," Kedrick said.

"Just say hello, then let him take a good look at you," Audubon said.

They stopped in front of 24–24½ Harland. Kedrick got out of the Studebaker, pushed the hair back from his forehead, but couldn't muster the courage to walk to the porch. "Go ahead," Audubon said. "Take your turn first."

Kedrick meandered up. Stepping onto the porch, he

looked in through the front window. It was true, the living room was set up just like his on Ash, except for the doilies on the chairs. There was a big Philco, a hassock. The outright familiarity of the room almost lulled Kedrick into thinking he was home.

Through the screen door he could see down the hallway into the kitchen. A tall, pretty woman with dark blond hair stood in the doorway. She was talking on the phone. Part of the cord was wrapped around her wrist like a snake bracelet, and she held almost perfectly still. She wore a beige silk-crepe dress, bone slingback shoes. Then, she turned to her left, her head held high in a stoic pose. Dahlia called such a posture "statuesque" when she and Kedrick looked at storefront mannequins once.

Evelyn—it had to be she—moved from the doorway. Dalton, who sat at the kitchen table, intently listened to the phone conversation. It was the first time Kedrick had seen him in clothes other than his conductor's uniform in a year. He looked sour and exhausted.

Looking at all of this, it wasn't so much that Evelyn had replaced Dahlia, or that this house had replaced the one on Ash, or Lapaz had replaced Mishawaka. It was that he felt caught between lives: he was confronting the almost familiar—the almost familiar father in the almost familiar house. He looked into the kitchen with his 3-D glasses on this time.

Evelyn hung up the phone. "Dalton, sweetie," she said. "That was Donna Roo. She and Harold are canceling hamburgers and the three-D movie, due to the tornado warning. Did you know about any tornado warning? I sure didn't. Who keeps track of such things, going about a busy life?"

Kedrick turned and faced the street. It was dusk, and the 3-D glasses made the maple tree loom twice its size. Slow as a tightrope walker, Kedrick made his way to the Studebaker, the glasses distorting whatever he looked at. He leaned in through the window, "He's home, but he's got company," Kedrick said.

"We'll come back another time," Audubon said.

Kedrick got in the front seat. "What'll we do now?" he said.

Audubon pointed to the lowering rain clouds on the horizon; a few last streaks of daylight shone through.

"Let's drive around in the storm a bit," Audubon said. "Then go back and watch the movie. The Savoy's our nighttime address, isn't it?"

Catching Heat

TROPICAL BENNY, A COCOA-BROWN TWO-YEAR-OLD, came up fast, and I caught heat. That's an old-time phrase, "catching heat," used in my line of work. I call trotting races. Leaning into the microphone, I announced, "Benny looks a solid first." I'd spoken for the future, then Benny lagged behind. The winner was Bourbon No Water, driven by Donny Malick.

A caller can get ahead of himself, ahead of the horses. Suddenly, midrace, he makes a prediction. He can falsely boost a spectator's hopes, someone who's privately placed a bet just because he likes the name of a horse or the way it struts. A caller should be obligated only to the moment. He has to demonstrate enthusiasm, certainly. But if a wayward spark of excitement hits, if emotions take over, he's caught heat. Like I did at the Barton summer fair.

Right after the race, Donny Malick stormed into the announcer's booth. I wondered if he'd even had time to stable his horse. "What in *hell* were you doing?" he said.

"What's bothering you, Donny? You won, didn't you?"

"You were rooting for a horse," Donny said. "I should bring an inquiry. I could get you fired. Tropical Benny didn't even *show*."

"I just caught heat, and you came in first," I said. "Pick up your thousand dollars and go home."

Donny stuffed his hands into his back pockets. "You know what?" he said. "Tonight, me and Abigail are going to park right on Danville Hill where Canada comes in on the radio." He looked at the floor.

"Get the fuck out."

Donny slowly lifted his face, so that it seemed that gravity itself drew his mouth into a scowl. "I predict that every time I'm on the track, you catch heat."

I turned my back on him, and Donny left the booth.

It had been a year since Donny and Abigail had taken up, but it still hurt. Abigail—I'd always called her Abby—and I had lived for five years in a ramshackle red Cape at the top of Danville Hill. Below was the village of Cabot, where the famous creamery is. Abby worked at Dunn's in Montpelier, dressing mannequins and designing storefront windows. On Thursdays before a weekend sale, she worked late.

Say we were out to a movie or visiting friends, we'd drive home down the Lower Cabot Road in my ten-year-old Buick. Actually, I'd always drive. Abby preferred to look out the window. She'd try to locate the outlines of cows, deer's eyes shining in the fields, owl faces on wooden fences. "Ghosties," she called such apparitions. Through the creamery windows, we could see workers on break, dressed like surgeons in white caps and gowns. We'd turn up Danville Hill, and then a mystical thing happened. Abby switched on the car radio. "Here comes Canada," she'd say.

Right there, halfway up the hill, a distant station waited for us. It was NWT, which should've been heard only by people in the Northwest Territories. I'm speaking here of not more than a ten-yard stretch of Danville Hill; no phone poles, no barbed wire, nothing but the night air to ricochet Canada into our radio. It was an eerie sort of privilege that Abby and I had always kept to ourselves—until she let Donny in on it.

It first happened the summer we'd moved in together. One night, we'd eaten dinner at Julio's Mexican Restaurant. Afterward, I stood out front and waited as Abby walked the few blocks to look at the gold dome of the capitol building. Then, we drove to Cabot. When we reached the hill, a local station had a Sousa march in progress. On the hill it was suddenly interrupted by: "Serving the remote communities in our northland." The announcer had a low, soothing voice. "It's a ghosty," Abby said. We parked on the side of the hill and listened to NWT until three A.M. Abbey grew pensive. "Is

155

there a time difference between north to south?" she asked. "That part of Canada is so far away. Seems like it's always earlier in the day up there. Maybe I'm thinking of snow and how it lights things up."

"No," I said, "time zones only run east to west."

"Well," she said, "they should change that."

Abby laughed wildly, not her usual soft laugh. "The ghost of a whole country wandered down," she said. "This is where it lives."

Mist packed the valley over the river in the first light; NWT played Sinatra ballads, and Abby looked sleepy-eyed. She was twenty-nine, tall, and had pale green eyes and dark red hair held up in barrettes but also falling down in curls. She was staring dreamily at the radio.

"You're hypnotized almost," I said. "Why not just move up to northern Canada, you're so drawn to it. I'd go. I'd go anywhere with you."

"No," she said. "If we moved to Canada, Canada wouldn't visit us. Not like it does here."

She snuggled close and said, "Want to see how I undress the mannequins?" She opened the top button of her magenta blouse. "You don't mind if a whole country listens in on us, do you?"

"I don't mind anything," I said.

"Keep the radio on, then," she said, slipping out of her jeans.

.   .   .

Each summer Abby came to the Barton fair, held during the second week in August. From my elevated booth, I'd catch a glimpse of her standing near the grandstand. While the trotters took their warm-up laps, she'd stop and wave until she caught my attention. I'd be getting things in order. I'd study the race program, pronounce the names of the horses to myself: China Lake, Easy Does It, Gabriel's Jazz, Home On Time, First Lily, and the like. I'd place the program on its stand, put my soft drinks in the cooler, change the coffee filter, set out an extra chair for Abby and one for old Dwight Hatch. Dwight was a retired caller. Even though his eyesight was terrible, he was a fixture in the booth. Sometimes during a race I'd notice him moving his mouth as though announcing the names of horses, but no words came out. I think he must've been remembering the names of dead horses, from races years back. Abby and Dwight liked each other. Dwight would ask me, "When are you two getting the wedding rings?"

From the booth, I'd see Abby appear and disappear into the midway. She'd try out the dart tosses and crazy mechanical rides with names that sounded like collisions were inevitable. She'd sit for hours in Cafe-in-a-Trailer, gossiping with Melanie, the owner and waitress. Later in the day, she'd watch the bandstand being constructed. She'd take in the details of how it was put together, the floor, the rivets, the Chinese lanterns hung from a wide rectangle of string. She found the lanterns romantic.

Around two o'clock, Abby would come to the announcer's booth, where she'd percolate some coffee and hand me a cup right away. Then she'd pour herself a glass of lemonade from the ice-filled pitcher. During a race she'd lean forward on her creaky foldup chair, all interest and delight at the event. She loved the actual races, but her favorite things were the acts in between. There'd be an organist behind a curtain, like at a baseball game: someone with very dramatic musical tastes. A hand flight up and down the keyboard, then a crescendo, and out would ride a shabby trio of chimps on tricycles, dressed in spangled shirts, lips pouted—one would be honking a big old-fashioned bicycle horn. Their trainers, a man and wife, would jog to midstage and take a long bow, sweeping the stage floor with their hats. They'd be wearing the same shirts as the chimps.

Then there'd be a hopeless comedian dressed in a baggy suit. I've forgotten his name—Maxwell something. Abby would mumble his jokes—"I'm a country singer, but no country will admit it!"

Then there'd be a man who did balancing acts. The simpler the stunt, the wilder the organ accompaniment. First, he'd stand on two hands, then on one, while his wife and two young daughters wearing Three Stooges masks poked at each other's eyes and whooped and chased in circles. Abby couldn't get over this act. She'd help Dwight to his feet, pull us both to the microphone, and make us applaud. She'd whistle, which echoed over the bandstand. "Bravo!" she'd yell. "Bravo!"

The last year or so Abby and I were together, we had our troubles. We had weeks in which we were angry, even fuming for no good reason, except that perhaps being angry was some kind of communication. I'd brought up marriage, and Abby always detoured around that subject. She'd begun to work late three or four times during the week. I realized it was to be away from me, but didn't know it was to be with Donny. She'd never mentioned him, even in passing. He lived on a tributary to the Lower Cabot Road. When the three of us ran into each other in town, they were always polite, civil, but I didn't feel a tension. They didn't glance away, which would have signaled something, as I knew them both to look directly into a person's face when they spoke. I was ignorant as a field mouse.

I knew little about Donny. I'd once shared a room with him, at the Motel 6 outside of Bangor, Maine. I'd been asked to call races at a winter fair. It was late March. The winter circuit ran until April and ended with Spring Fest, in Orono, Maine, which invited drivers from the Canadian Maritimes as well. I recognized Donny from Cabot, of course, and when I saw him in the diner outside of Bangor, I said, "Look, I'm a little short of cash. You mind sharing a room? I'm calling tomorrow's races." He seemed nervous, but agreed to it. But a strange thing happened. The minute we stepped into the motel room, Donny tore a page from the Gideon's Bible and lit it with a cigar. At first, this made me laugh. But then I said, "Where I come from, that's a sacrilege." Of course, Donny and I were raised in neighboring towns, he in Hardwick, me in Cabot.

He sat down on the bed, staring at me, nodding his head. He smoked without talking, blew a few smoke rings. "Can you show Abigail a good time, considering the money you make?" he said.

"What do you know about it?" I said, suddenly offended.

"Just curious," he said. "We're being roommates here. I wanted to ask something important."

"Well, we're not friends," I said. "We're just splitting a bill."

That was our entire conversation. Though it was only nine o'clock, I got into my bed. I heard Donny go out. I heard him come back again in the middle of the night. We ate separate breakfasts at the diner. I paid for my half of the room, then drove out to the fair. That afternoon, Bourbon No Water broke stride in the first race, and Donny had to maneuver him off the track. In the fifth race, he came in third. So Donny took home $250. I said to myself, Donny's a good driver, but I don't like him. That day, I'd called the trotters as well as I ever had. Their names struck me as poetry.

A few weeks later, in early April, Abby and I were sitting at night in our kitchen. The dishes had already been washed, and I was about to have a cognac, which I did at least twice a week. At the table, Abby was leafing through a volume of the *Encyclopedia Britannica*. "David," she said, in a sweeter tone than I'd heard in some time, "do you know which volume I'm up to?"

"I wish I did, but I don't."

"I'm up to the H," she said. "The H volume. And I'm very upset, near to crying. Do you know why?"

"Tell me."

"Because I've just read about horse latitudes," she said. "Have you heard of them?"

"No, Abby, I haven't."

"It's a real place from history," she said. "Golfo de las Yeguas. It's where some ships carrying horses to the New World were caught in the middle of the ocean because there were no winds to fill their sails. So they drifted for weeks. And pretty soon everyone was hungry. They had to lead the horses off the ships. Jettison, it's called. Into the sea. To make the ships lighter, so a smaller breeze could take them somewhere."

"Did it work?"

"That's not the point," she said. "The point is, I'm angry at those people. How could they do such a thing, to God's beautiful creatures? I mean, just imagine it."

"If it actually happened, then you don't have to imagine it."

"Yes you do. It was in another century. Not being there, you have to imagine it."

"Don't worry, Abby. Take Bermingham's horses across the road, for instance. The ones you see every day. They aren't going to drown. They'll be all right."

Abby was lightly sobbing by this time. "I'm just thankful they're surrounded by land," she said. "All safe and sound away from drowning."

The notion calmed her, and a kind of patchwork tenderness sprung up between us.

"Well," she said suddenly, "I'm going to the store. A sale starts tomorrow, so I've got to get started on the windows."

She walked out to the driveway, to her old Fairlane. Its muffler was secured by wire, the upholstery bandaged with masking tape. There was no radio. But it got her to Montpelier and back. Anyway, that was the kind of good-bye we'd been saying, no good-bye, really, and no good-bye kiss.

I waited up, but Abby was much later than usual. I phoned the department store without luck. I decided to drive in to Montpelier to see if Abby was all right. On average it was a forty-minute drive, but I made it in twenty-five. The streets were empty. I was about to turn into the alley alongside Dunn's, when I saw Abby in the window and Donny Malick out front on the sidewalk. Driving past, I parked in the lot behind the fire department, then walked to where I could stand unnoticed. Donny was staring transfixed while Abby did a kind of striptease. The window was brightly lit. She kept her own clothes on, but was slowly, button by button, snap by snap, undressing a mannequin. The crazy thing was, the handsome male mannequin with perfectly chiseled features had on exactly the same outfit as Donny. It was a sale of western-style clothes: cowboy boots, jeans, checkered shirts, jean jackets with corduroy collars, leather belts with wide, metal buckles. I remembered Donny's belt. It had buffalo-head nickels encased in it all around.

I drove home in a storm of jealousy and betrayal. At two A.M., Abby still wasn't home. It was impossible to sleep. My thinking took one bad turn after the other. Having witnessed their sleazy rendezvous, I knew it was over between Abby and me. I suspected that she'd seen my car and didn't have the heart to face me at home. This thought made it worse, because I then imagined her at Donny's house. The night drew me out onto the porch. I heard Bermingham's horses running in the dark. When I started to walk down the hill, they came over for a look, snorting, nuzzling at the fence.

With each step, my misery rose. I had a demon in me. And then I saw the truck. The moon had come out. It was Donny's truck, a battered Chevy with a trailer hitch and no hubcaps. It was too late to keep from being seen, if they were looking. Drawing closer, I heard NWT. It was a shock to realize another radio could pick it up. It simply had never occurred to me before. There was a news report on. Nothing much to make love to. I saw two bodies pressed to each other, and it stopped me cold. In a burst, I threw two rocks at the windshield. And nothing happened. The couple didn't move. I walked to the truck and opened a door. Two fully dressed mannequins were in an embrace. This cruelty made me yank the mannequins out and pitch them at the roadside. Then I got in to the truck and saw the keys hanging in the ignition, so I drove without headlights to a patch of gravel about ten yards into an access road for tractors. I lost NWT. I sat in the cab a while, smelling Abby's perfume, its aroma mixed with harness oil and cigar smoke. I turned off the radio, then the ignition, and walked up the hill. Around dawn, I fell asleep in my kitchen, slumped over the table.

The garbage collector, Zack Almanting, woke me up, banging on my screen door. "Dave—you want these or what?" I sat up and saw that Zack was holding the mannequins. "Found these two dead on the road," he said. "I know that Abby dresses these things." He held the mannequins forward as if he were about to introduce them. "This one here's got a decent shirt my size, if you don't mind."

"It's yours."

"Hey, you all right?"

"Just do me a favor, okay? Take the shirt, then crush those mannequins in your truck."

"Fair exchange," Zack said.

Two weeks later, when I was calling trotters in New Hampshire, Abby moved in with Donny. I returned to a house empty of her possessions. It all left me sullen, heartsick. But

I continued calling trotters; for a good while, it was all that was familiar.

That August, I caught heat at the Barton fair; Donny stomped in and out of the announcer's booth.

Donny and Abby continued to park on Danville Hill. I drove home up the opposite side of the hill. I didn't even grocery shop in Cabot anymore.

The last day of August, I drove Dwight Hatch to the fairgrounds in Bangor. As I read the program, I was relieved to see that Bourbon No Water wasn't entered. But then, just before the second race, I looked directly across the track and spotted Donny and Abby standing at the rail, where they knew I'd see them. I thought they might be touring Maine on their honeymoon. At that moment, I felt in control. Abby's deceptions, knowing she lived with Donny, rarely poisoned my soul or made my heart cringe the way they had at first. "Just do your work," I said to myself. Far to my right, the pace truck sped up and swung off the track, stopping next to the emergency exit, where an ambulance was parked. I saw Will Bellevance, the driver, crouch out and walk toward the midway. The sulkies came by, and I announced, clearly and steadily, how they were placed. Easy Does It was in the lead.

The second lap went smoothly. But as the sulkies rounded the final curve, it was like a wave pouring over me. I stared at Donny and Abby. She was touching his face. My mind drifted; I pictured the bandstand, the paper lanterns, the band, and heard a slow song in my head. I pictured Abby and Donny dancing. I saw their belts touch. I felt her pressed against me, but imagined her with him. Off to my right, I vaguely sensed the horses. "Dave," Dwight Hatch said, "get your binoculars up and voice going." But I stared at Donny and Abby.

Dwight slapped me on the back, and I snapped to and announced Easy Does It was still leading. But I'd spoken for the past, because when the sulkies finished, Easy Does It was third. I swung my binoculars back to the rail. Abby was laughing. Donny, too. I leaned into the microphone and said loudly, in quick, evenly spaced words: "Abby-don't-you-laugh!" I had startled myself and looked to Dwight for some help. But he was blinking, confused. His face right up against the race program, he ran his finger down the page, looking for a horse by that name.

Milk Train

ON OCTOBER 7, 1912, AN HOUR AFTER TRAIN #2204 DE-
railed, Second Engineer Corbett Ingham woke facedown in
milk. The wreckage had the look of dinosaurs in battle. It was
a frozen instant, all the screeching and friction stilled. The
locomotive and first milk car were heaved up against each
other, leaving room for a man to walk underneath. The second milk car was on its side. The heavy round hoods of its
silos had snapped off like bottle caps. Milk gushed out with
pulmonary force—gallons and gallons, so that creamy white
tributaries meandered toward the creek thirty or so feet away.

Just prior to being hurtled out, Corbett had dozed off on
the caboose's slat bunk, an issue of *Crime* open on his chest.
He liked to sleep with the door propped open, the crisp au-

tumn air drawn in by the train's movement, a single blanket spread over him, the collar of his flannel shirt buttoned so he wouldn't wake to a sore throat. In early October, as it was, blood-colored leaves were drying, oranges, yellows, browns— all the oaks, maples, and birch blazing and darkening at once. Skunk cabbage ripened the air along the marshes.

It had been an exhausting day, beginning at 5:30 A.M., when he'd arrived at the Bennington, Vermont, depot. He'd first helped Chief Engineer Jake Charyn supervise the loading of milk. A dozen dairy farmers had their milk wagons and trucks lined up. He'd then hosed down the locomotive, two refrigerated cars and caboose. Next he caught up on paperwork. The train set out at 10:15 A.M. There was no work for Corbett until they reached Montpelier. In the caboose, he placed his shoes next to a lantern on the shelf. He'd read halfway through "The Case of the Missing Nanny" when the ticking of the wheels began to lull him to sleep; he put down his magazine.

Milk, the unmistakable feel and smell of it, woke Corbett. He dug his fingers into the earth as if to keep his grip on the planet. His head hurt, his ears thrummed deep inside, he thought his heart was wedging in extra beats. He opened both eyes, but one was pressed to the ground. With the other he focused on a reddish blur just a few yards away, until its edges sharpened enough so that Corbett saw it was a fox lapping up milk. Corbett heard the fox's tongue working. This was a shabby animal, its rust fur tinged with gray, its ribs showing.

The only evidence of former health was a somewhat luxuriant tail ruffling in the wind. It seemed to Corbett that it was somehow wrong for this fox to be so near. He always had known foxes to be jittery animals, scared off by the clatter of a fallen rake or clap of the hands. It seemed wrong that milk had drawn a wild animal from the woods. He saw the fox look over; it caught the scent of helplessness.

A sickening pain branched along Corbett's ribs, bringing tears to his eyes. He flinched, and although he was flat on the ground his brain said he was falling. The sky spun, and Corbett blacked out. When he woke again, milk had crusted on his face and on the weeds around him. He took this as evidence that time had passed. He looked for the fox, but it was gone. Then again, he couldn't be certain that it was ever there. He recalled a reassuring habit. Every day he'd feel his own pulse, at the neck or wrist. Now, he opened his eyes and lifted his hand to his neck. He thought to stand up.

Whether the fox had been flesh or vision, at least it hadn't been an emissary from the hereafter come to lap up his soul. Corbett laughed, a little celebration that made his insides detonate. He held still until the pain subsided. Then he inched along the ground, managing to reach a clump of grass. Lightly, he brushed the dirt from his eyelids, then bit away the grass, chewed, grimaced, and swallowed. It tasted of rancid milk, and he began to choke. Realizing that his actions were desperate, he tried to stay calm, to breathe evenly if not deeply and focus on staying alive. He wondered what happened to Frank, Haj, and Freddy, the inspectors from the main station in town. In his four years of working the milk route, Corbett had seen two wrecks. Not wrecks he'd personally been in; ones he'd gone out to with the inspectors. Touring wrecks he felt was just another part of his commitment to railroading, which was most of his world. Even on his days off, he'd hang around the station with the telegraph operator, brakemen, and inspectors, drinking coffee and eating doughnuts. Corbett had grown up among train men because his father was a dairy farmer. As he got older, he'd picked up details of train work, how to inventory freight, file invoices, draw up schedules. At fifteen, he was apprenticed to Jake Charyn and at sixteen hired on.

He lived alone in the Bixby Hotel, in a shabby room on the first floor. Whenever he was there for even a few hours, things would somehow fall into disorder. His precious true crime stories were strewn on the floor near the bed, in the bathroom, on the night table, even though there was a bookshelf. The depot was his true home, a place of order; the hotel was where he slept. He sent his laundry out to Mrs. Peters, sister of Mr. Phelps, the hotel's owner. She stacked his shirts, trousers, and underwear on the dresser. Corbett would take these as needed, without ever putting them in the closet or drawers. Soiled clothes were tossed into a corner. He ate most of his meals in the hotel's restaurant, though on Sundays he had dinner at his parents' house. He'd never been out of Vermont.

Corbett was just under six feet tall, with a combative stance, though he'd always hated to fight. In conversation he'd draw his face back in doubt, even before the other person had spoken. This was a gesture of shyness that some mistook for rudeness, yet Corbett was aware that the two could be one and the same. He smoked a cigar after each meal. First he chewed on it, rotating it in his mouth, working the saliva stain halfway down its length. This was more or less in imitation of his father, Lytton, who warned him about his boyish face and said that smoking a cigar would help him to be accepted among men. But mostly his cigar-smoking habits caused the other trainmen to snicker.

He had a woman friend, Rose, who was ten years older and who taught school in Burlington. History and grammar were her subjects, but her heart was in painting. Rose was a miniaturist, and Corbett had a number of her works in a shoebox in the hotel. She was pretty, but pale, and wore pale collared blouses. She kept her dark brown curls short and tightly spooled. The curls, cut evenly all around, reminded Corbett of window shades that could snap up at any moment.

Corbett had dinner with Rose every Thursday, on his overnight in Burlington. He stayed at the Hanley Guest House there. They ate at Voigts Restaurant, which overlooked Lake Champlain. For a chaperone, Rose always brought her younger sister, Evie, who looked like a thinner, slightly unkempt version of Rose, though with deep red hair. Once, when the waiter came to the table holding a tall, dark-grained pepper shaker with a metal grinder at one end, Evie said almost under her breath, "I like this restaurant because they serve pepper with a bassoon." Rose didn't laugh, but the waiter did, though his smile was pained. Corbett loved the way that Evie offered up a private thought so shyly. After dinner, when he was back in his room, he often tried to understand his feelings. Out loud he'd say, "I like Evie more. So what am I doing?" It was a question he never knew how to answer.

At dinner, Rose would read Corbett descriptions of romantic heroes proposing marriage to beautiful heroines. These made Corbett not a little uneasy. He knew Rose was trying to tell him something, but couldn't see what the proposals had to do with life outside the books. Rose read dramatically, wagging a finger above the table as if she were scolding a pupil. Sometimes she'd underline a sentence in the air before drawing an exclamation point on the tablecloth with her finger. With her other hand, she'd press the prong end of a fork to the back of Corbett's hand to keep his attention. When Rose closed her book, the waiter would serve her and Evie tea, and Corbett would have coffee. One evening, after a particularly long reading, he turned to Evie, who stared at her clenched napkin, her expression suggesting the deepest embarrassment. Of course, Corbett knew she was secretly pleased at his attentions to her.

"I'd never propose like that," he said, his voice wavering and his eyes still trained on Evie. "No, I'd just say, 'I've built a house. There's room for you there. Anything you want. I work on a milk train.' " For Corbett it was an unguarded moment. Evie quickly drank her entire glass of ice water, then drank her sister's, too. Corbett moved his own water glass nearer to Evie, but she refused it.

Once, at the beginning of dinner, Rose read a sentence that hushed them all for the rest of their meal: "A broken heart is always somebody's fault."

Sprawled by the tracks, the evening's chill working into him, Corbett wasn't thinking of Evie or Rose. He wasn't thinking forward or back. Pain and a growing anger kept him to the present. The inspectors should've realized by now that something was wrong. The relay officer north of Bennington should've wired the main depot when the train didn't pass on schedule. They should've traced it, puzzled out the delay. Haj—he was the strongest—should be pumping the hand-cart's handle, hurrying them all on out. They'd be wearing black suits, black hats, and black shoes, just like undertakers.

And Willis T. White, the famous catastrophe photographer, should be with them or arrive shortly. White lived in Bennington, but he'd been all over the world. He'd witnessed earthquakes, photographed long cracks in the earth that were later put on maps. He'd been in monsoons, shot many-colored geese swimming above rooftops. His house contained mementos of all sorts of human calamities. He'd written his memoirs and was retired, except for continuing to photograph train wrecks. In the past five years there'd been eight wrecks in New England. It was a hobby the train routes provided for.

Corbett had always liked seeing White around town, in his peaked hat, breeches, and embroidered vests. And of course he'd never be without his three-legged stool, because he was almost a dwarf. His complexion had an aggressive ruddiness, almost a rash. And he wore white gloves, all year round. Corbett had never seen White bare-handed, though one time he almost had. White had stepped out of the bathhouse next to the Bixby Hotel wearing a striped bathing suit, and he was just pulling on his gloves. The gloves made everyone wonder about White's hands. Perhaps they'd been mangled in one of the catastrophes he'd photographed, or scarred by spilled chemicals in his dark room.

Pain toured Corbett's body fast, outlining it the way lightning illuminates a coastline at night. Then, the smell of burned milk snapped in his nostrils. But the train wasn't on fire; milk wasn't boiling in its cars. This was a memory.

One summer's day when Corbett was ten, he walked over to visit his grandmother Christa, a silent woman whom he adored and visited every day. Christa had accidentally shot her husband, Llewyn, a blacksmith and glassblower, who was Corbett's step-grandfather. She'd killed him with a deer rifle and had been punished by gossip ever since. The church threw her out as if she'd done it on purpose. "One day I might've done it on purpose," she'd confided to Corbett while they were eating pie. "But the accident happened first."

It was a humid day, and Corbett, his feet callused from walking barefoot, was carrying a nasty surprise: a catfish skull with a whitened bone grin and flaps of skin attached to each side. The skull lay on a bed of assorted chocolates, which Corbett had bought at the apothecary with his allowance. He'd unwrapped the box, placed the skull under the doily, then taped the box shut again, tying the ribbon into a bow.

Corbett was angry at his grandmother—that was the reason for all of this. The week before, he'd overheard his father telling his mother that the railroad had come to an agreement: they planned to lay tracks through the east section of Cutter's farm and on out, which would put them right through Christa's house. They'd surveyed and figured that would take the least dynamiting. But Christa just wouldn't abide. She out-and-out refused. "I just now went over to see her," said Lytton. "I walked all the way over there, and she slammed the door in my face. Then she opened it and slammed it again. The railroad'll pay to move her house and then some. They promised her that. But she wouldn't hear any of it."

"When is this supposed to happen?" asked Corbett's mother.

"A week," Lytton said. "Christa says she'll tie herself to something in her kitchen. Maybe the stove."

Corbett took this to mean that Christa would actually remain in her house as the train crashed through. He never stopped to wonder how this could happen without tracks inside Christa's house. He was just struck dumb at the thought that she didn't care about him enough to stay alive. After a period of brooding, his temper flared, and he refused to visit. A whole week had gone by before he thought up his revenge.

As he neared Christa's house, he was startled to see that a dozen workmen had laid siege to the place. The house, jacked up, was separated from its porch. Most of the men sat on a flatbed truck, eating sandwiches and drinking from thermos bottles. Dropping the chocolates, Corbett ran toward the house. "Get goddamn away from there!" one man yelled. "That house could fall on you. And that old coot inside's got a rifle!" But Corbett ducked down under the porch and, all but breaststroking over the dirt, got himself to the front door. Hoisting himself up, he jammed splinters into his palms.

Once inside, he brushed himself off and looked down the hall toward the kitchen. Christa stood at the woodstove. "Mind you sweep up that mess you've brought in," she said. Corbett looked around for the broom but couldn't find it. Then he noticed piles of dirt everywhere, from the flower pots that had fallen over. As he walked down the hall, he saw that the beds, dressers, and tables had all slid against the left-side walls. They no doubt had jacked up the right side of the house first.

"Hello, Grandma," Corbett said. It was the first time that he'd seen his grandmother without her hair coiled up on top of her head. It just fell in long, matted strands. Christa was heating a pan full of milk at the stove and, like a lumberjack, had tied herself to it. Her departed husband's asbestos gloves were wedged between the rope and the stove to keep the rope from burning. Soon the milk began to scald, rising quickly and spilling over. Its acrid smell filled the kitchen. But Corbett ignored the milk because Christa did, and said, "Grandma, they're moving your house so the train won't kill you!"

"Don't worry about me," Christa said. "Do you want to get inside the rope with me?"

But in the next few moments the workmen stormed in, lifting Christa and Corbett out, relaying them like gunnysacks. Once in view of the hoists and pulleys and the truck, Corbett cried out, "Grandma, don't watch!"

Christa slapped his face. "We have to look," she said. "How else will we know exactly what happened? Even if nobody else cares, we can tell each other."

As the workmen attended to final details, Christa gripped Corbett's hand in her own, letting go only when the house was loaded on the flatbed. They watched the house moving down the makeshift road toward town. All that was left behind was the porch. "Guess those men won't be back for it until tomorrow," Christa said. "Go and sit on it if you want."

Corbett took this as a request, which he quickly obeyed. From the porch he watched his grandmother walk into the woods, squat down, lifting her dress slightly. When she came back she said, "They just made me do something I haven't done since I was a little girl."

The smell of burned milk hung in the air, where the house had been. "Rotten," Corbett said, "like a skunk." He hoped the smell plagued the workmen the rest of their lives.

Several hours into the darkness, the inspectors still hadn't arrived. Corbett raised himself up and felt as if he were lifting an ox. He stood and managed to hold his balance, then took a few steps over to the train. Leaning against the locomotive, just where the cow-catcher had gouged into the ground, his lungs cringed; each breath yanked at a rib. He thought: I might be dying inside myself. When they find me, I'll be like a grain sack full of rain.

He said a prayer out loud, asking to live. Its emotion pitched high, this was about as righteous as Corbett had ever gotten . . . until he realized it wasn't a prayer at all. Instead, he'd spoken the exact words Detective Mariposa had used in his cowardly, whining, down-on-his-knees begging to a kidnap murderer holding a pistol to his head in "The Case of the Missing Nanny."

Then, out of nowhere, or the train or woods, he heard: "What kind of phony prayer was that?"

"Who's there?" Corbett shouted.

"I talk with too much effort, I'll die in the next minute."

"What? Jake—is that you?"

Jake Charyn was a youthful fifty, his broad chest and shoulders always pulled back as if he were inhaling. He was so expansive in his gestures that Corbett couldn't imagine him buckled over, pinned inside the locomotive as he had to have been.

"Get me some milk," Jake said, his voice weak but distinct.

"Milk? I don't understand."

It exhausted Corbett as well, to be talking through the double darkness of night and locomotive iron. He wondered if Jake was on his back, if he could see the few stars directly above.

"*Milk*, Second Engineer," Jake said, louder this time. He coughed; a wheeze up a broken throat. Then Corbett heard a burning hiss like a small steam valve opening. The sound could've come from Jake or the train. "I'm parched," Jake said, his voice rallying. "And Walter Till's dead in here with me." Till was the coal shoveler. "He won't be having any milk. Corbett, listen to me. I want to taste some milk."

Corbett began to sob. "The thing is . . ." He choked it back. "There is no milk. It's gone."

"Corbett, we're hauling a ton of milk."

"The milk's spilled. It's gone down into the creek. What hasn't, I can't get to. I have broken ribs."

"Corbett?"

"Jake, anyway it's dark now. I'm sorry."

"Never mind. Listen. You don't have much of a life. I'm saying this right in front of poor Mr. Till, Corbett, go and marry Till's wife."

"What are you saying, Jake?"

"Get on over, soon as you're up to it. Soon as she's over her grief. And marry Alice Till. You ever see her?"

"No, I never did."

"Then you're in for a surprise. Imagine a dying man saying somebody else's in for a surprise! But you are." Jake hacked, then groaned. "She's just twenty-three."

"Listen, Jake, I do too have a life."

"The hell you do. All you have is that stinking hotel. That stinking tittering girl up in Burlington, and her stinking sister. You consider that a life? That supper you keep having with them's a cesspool, and you're sinking deeper and deeper. Corbett—my last words are Alice Till."

"I'll get you some help."

"Just get away from my train. I want this place for myself."

Corbett stumbled backward and rolled down an incline. He didn't stop until he jammed up against a stump. Small stones pressed to his face. He heard the creek close by. He edged to it. He lay still a moment. Then, cupping up water, he tasted milk.

He didn't die down there, in the silt and autumn mushrooms and rock outcroppings. The sound of the creek connected night to morning. He struggled to his feet, more or less clawing his way up the slope. At the top, he stood again and made his way toward the train, cracking small, frozen puddles of milk with each step. Dropping to one knee, he rested. A few more steps, and he was back at the train. He stretched himself out in front of the wreck and only then fell into a restless sleep.

When he lifted his head, it was full daylight. He saw something slowly walking toward him down the middle of the tracks. It was the fox all right, the one from the day before. Ignoring him again, it found an opening in the wreckage and disappeared.

I'm going to die here; that fox will be the last thing to see me alive, though I might be the last one to see him alive, too. The way he looked, the train might be his grave.

Corbett's thinking began to fade, but then he heard a whoop down the tracks, like an animal sound: a highly pitched note with an echo. In a few moments there was more whooping, and Corbett saw the inspectors. He was utterly surprised and more angry than ever. Haj furiously pumped the railcart's handle, and sitting as regally as could be managed on his three-legged stool was Willis T. White, his tripod camera flying a white handkerchief flag. To either side were Frank and Freddy, each riding an old plow horse that hardly lifted its hooves.

"Jesus save us all, the bastards," Corbett mumbled, more to himself and the fox than anyone else.

At the sight of Corbett, the men stopped about twenty yards away. Frank and Freddy climbed down and dug flasks out of their satchels. They each took long swigs. Haj stood up straight on the cart, while White remained seated.

"Where in hell you been?" Corbett shouted, then fell back to the tracks.

Immediately Haj rushed over, tilted Corbett's head back, and gave him some whiskey. "Just a little now, fella," he said.

Suddenly, the fox darted from under the caboose right past Corbett and toward the handcart. Freddy picked up a crowbar and yelled, "Tally ho!" swinging it in the air. The fox spun around and ran back to the train. Freddy ran to the locomotive and began whacking and ringing the crowbar against it, trying to scare up the fox. He walked along the wreck, every so often crouching down to look under, and once shouting, "Come on out, you sorry excuse for one of God's creatures. Come on out and meet your maker!"

Spitting whiskey, Corbett said, "Tell him to stop that. Jake's dead in there. So is Mr. Till. It's wrong, what he's doing. It's just . . ." and he fell back.

Freddy kept up his harangue, despite Frank and Haj screaming at him to stop. He worked his way to the caboose, whose one unbroken window he smashed with the crowbar. Having given up on Freddy, both Haj and Frank were now climbing over the locomotive, peering in through its door. When they saw Jake and Mr. Till, both stood up straight. Frank crossed himself, mumbling a prayer.

"Hey, boys! Look up here!" White called out.

Willis was set; one hand held the powder tray, the other gripped the shutter squeeze.

"Now, Frank," White said, "just open up your suit coat a

little. And put your hand in one pocket. Haj, you hold out your watch, like you're registering the exact time of day. Come on, boys, let's have a nice pose. You're about to become history."

Whatever Lola Wants

HARRY CHAPPEL LOOKED IN HIS CLOSET. HE OWNED about thirty Hawaiian shirts, all sorts of patterns: grass huts, spearfishermen, torch ginger, pineapples, outrigger canoes, orchids, volcano goddesses. Each shirt was made of rayon, some had coconut-husk buttons. Lola had given him every last one. His favorite, a magenta silk screen with white palm trees, was a replica of the shirt Montgomery Clift died in at the end of *From Here to Eternity*. Harry had it on under his flannel pajama top.

"You slept in the Monty Clift!" Lola shouted from the kitchen. Harry heard pancakes being made, the scrape of the spatula. "How many do you want?"

"Just two," Harry said. "Two will be fine, what with the syrup." The shirt felt a little tight.

Harry considered a shirt with a breadfruit pattern on a rose background. It was the first shirt Lola had given him; that was twenty-two years ago, in 1943. Jon Hall wore one like it in that year's film fiasco, *White Savage*, which also starred Maria Montez and the cinnamon-skinned boy, Sabu. Out loud Harry gave his usual epitaph for the movie: "Down the toilet. And that set designer, the homo bastard, what's his name? *Lorenzo*, the man was obviously afraid to use his last name. No brains. Couldn't beat a chicken at checkers. To this day, I *still* cannot believe him and you, Lola. It turns my stomach."

Lola held the spatula above the frying pan and counted to ten. She figured that Harry was looking at the Jon Hall, because it always brought on a spell of ranting. "I've told you a thousand times," Lola said, now standing in the kitchen doorway, batter hardening on the spatula. "Nothing went on between him and me. Zero. Maybe that's what gets you, Harry. Would you be happier if something had happened? Then you could add an extra misery to the fact he fired you. Harry, you were a jealous man even before I met you. Do we have to go through it all again? I've got pancakes going here."

Harry chose an orange shirt with a surfer on each pocket, took off his pajama top, then the Monty Clift, put the fresh shirt on and a knit sweater over that. He took off his pajama bottoms and put on long underwear, trousers, socks, and goosedown slippers. "It's freezing out," he said toward the kitchen. Lola had gone back to the stove. "Weatherman says down to zero tonight, maybe fifteen below, what with the wind chill. I nearly froze getting the paper this morning, just to the porch and back."

"Poor thing," Lola said.

He gazed at the shirts again. "More than twelve years since we left Los Angeles," he said. "Can you believe it?"

The closet was a tropical place compared with what Harry saw out his back window. The upper Vermont valley, between Camel's Hump and Onion River, seemed locked in ice. There was a gray horizon, birch and pines outlined in snow. One crow flapping across the sky. The radiator in the house made dungeon clanks; Harry placed his hands on the cold glass. "And it's only March," he said.

"What?" Lola said. "I can't hear you."

"It's only March!" Harry shouted.

"You're good with facts," she said. "Always were."

"Maybe we should take a little tour out west," Harry said. "What do you think?"

"I was getting worried about you, Harry," Lola said.

"Why's that?" Harry said.

"Just that it's kind of late for you to be saying let's go west," Lola said. "Usually you say it in January. Every year you forget how much you hate L.A. The snow must give you amnesia. Ten minutes back there, you'd turn the car around and drive home. Come on in, Harry. I finished the pancakes."

"Not hungry," Harry said, glaring at the thermometer just outside the window. Before sitting down on his overstuffed brown chair and propping his feet on the matching hassock, he turned up the heat. Leaning back in the chair, he began to brood about *White Savage*. Lola set the table for herself.

In *White Savage*, Jon Hall, a popular actor at the time, ventured into the unknown reaches of a snake and voodoo jungle in order to save both Maria Montez and her friend, a bit part played by Lola. Both women had been kidnapped by savages. Throughout the movie, the muscular Hall, with his dark, deep-set eyes, revealed his discomfort with the role by continually adjusting his pith helmet. He just could not get the thing to sit right. The set, situated on a Hollywood back lot, was cluttered with electric cables and junction boxes. On the third day of shooting, a pet store iguana bit through a wire; heart-singed, it fell over. The lizard was easily replaced, of course, but the nature of the accident suggested the prevailing lack of authenticity. Chicanos played South Sea natives.

At age twenty-five, Harry was seriously flatfooted, which made it look like his feet both anchored him and propelled him forward with some effort. That, along with his weak ankles—he couldn't, for instance, roller-skate—kept him out of the army. But the war did afford him a start to his film career. He found work as an assistant to a director of propaganda films. Their job was to alternate cameo appearances of various movie stars into a sequence of battle footage, as if the stars were making "on the spot" reports. That was where Harry got his technical background. He was an electrical engineering student at USC when he landed a job as assistant set designer under Lorenzo on *White Savage*. It was his first Hollywood picture. He would, he figured, start out in set design, possibly working his way to directing. At the time he'd been studying Gauguin's strategies of light and color and thought day and night about the Tahitian paintings. He sat in the library for hours, paging through monographs on the French painter. With Gauguin as inspiration, Harry filled sketchbooks with complete sets: island horizons and dusks, bamboo light, thatched roofs dripping rain. He envisioned an Eden tinged with menace, a lush, timeless place in which, cannibals or no, Maria Montez would perish with grace. Working up his nerve with a few shots of bourbon, he presented his work to Lorenzo.

Lorenzo, waving away a young woman who had brought him coffee, had Harry flip the pages of his sketchbook as they stood midset. Lorenzo ran his hand through his hair. Then he sighed, "Look, Harry, I'm awfully tired. Fed up. Sabu's been a real pain. The picture's weeks behind schedule. I'm at my wit's end. This is no time for Polynesian porno paintings. For now just do what you're told."

Harry grabbed the notebook and punched Lorenzo in the forehead, where he'd aimed. Before Lorenzo, who'd been spun hard to his right, could regain his composure, Harry said, "I'm fired," and stalked off the set. Up until that mo-

ment—twice in the commissary, a few times on the set—
Harry and Lola had only exchanged glances. But glances can
have a lot of variety; they can be conversations. Both Harry
and Lola were conscious of a mutual interest. Now, on his
way out, he detoured over to Lola, who had seen the one-
punch battle. "I'll be on the Venice pier for a few days," he
said.

Harry stepped out of the set hangar into the sun, shaded
his eyes to get his bearings, then caught a bus to the pier,
which was his hangout. He knew a lot of people there, all
fishermen. Near the beach end of the pier was a concession
stand and a bait-and-tackle shop. There he bought a fold-up
bamboo rod and a plastic bucket full of squid bait. He walked
out to the end, sea wind in his face, and began fishing and
chatting with friends. His knuckles throbbed, but he was a
happy man. His sketchbooks were protected by his parka,
which lay folded on the pier, well away from the edge. For
two solid days he fished and drank his friend's rum and coffee,
and ate hamburgers from the concession. Twice he bought
popcorn, tossing most of the kernels to the perch and sea bass
minnows. He slept leaning up against a wooden pier stan-
chion.

Following Harry's abrupt departure from the set, Lola still
had two days' work. On the second day she'd been impaled
by a spear—for nine takes—and lashed to the sinuous trunk
of a jungle tree. ("I heard the first take was perfect," Harry
jealously complained years later. "He just liked seeing you

strapped to the tree.") When Hall and Sabu finally found Lola, she was a mere skeleton. In fact, they only knew it was Lola from her blouse. Considering that her abduction had taken place only the night before, her disintegration had occurred remarkably fast.

Altogether Lola had worked on the movie for five days; she wasn't an "extra," so she received thirty-five dollars a day, scale. And she got to keep the tangerine-colored blouse that both she and the skeleton had worn. The morning after her final shoot, she woke in her small apartment, bathed, and sewed up the spear hole in the blouse. Then she ironed the blouse, put it on with yellow slacks and flats, and took a bus to the pier. Harry was right where he'd said he would be.

From the moment she had first noticed him on the set, she had found Harry—with his light green eyes, thick brown hair, and nervous smile—the most attractive man she'd ever seen. Yet on the pier that morning she found him disheveled, hung over. His T-shirt was smeared with fish guts, and he was stretched out, his head on his parka, a small Chinese boy poking him in the belly, then running to the opposite side of the pier, shrieking laughter. Lola nudged Harry with her foot. "Go away, Peter Lin," Harry muttered, his eyes closed. "I'm taking a nap." Lola spilled some water from the bucket on his face, wiping her hands on his parka and backing up a few steps. When Harry looked up he said, "You're still thin"— referring to the movie skeleton, a scene he knew was in the script—"but you've made a miraculous recovery."

Lola, who had stolen the shirt Jon Hall had worn the day Harry struck Lorenzo, had brought it with her. She held it out to him. "Here," she said, "wear this. You're a mess."

Lola's real name was Lillian Applefeld; she changed it to Lola Field in 1940 on the morning of her first audition, for a small part she didn't get. She phoned her few friends and told them she'd changed it, wrote her parents in New Jersey for the same reason, and got a new driver's license. Three years later, when she met Harry, she was twenty-six, with curly black hair that she usually wore held back by red or white fake-jeweled combs on the right side. Her smile was nice, but she had two crooked front teeth she could never afford to get straightened, and finally didn't want to. "Pretty teeth don't matter for the parts I get," she once remarked. If the light was just so, Lola's face revealed Slavic features, something eastern Russian, perhaps Tartar. She had a way of framing her high cheekbones with her hands, sometimes kneading them, a habit that revealed her constant jitteriness. Hers was an open, friendly face, but she had a quick temper, a way of abruptly turning her head and staring at her own shoulder.

By the time she had quit acting in 1953, Lola had appeared in more than forty pictures. Her total time on the screen, however, was only seventy minutes or thereabouts. The time spent auditioning, loitering around sets, and in makeup, compared with those few minutes in the shadows or background of the limelight, was to Lola one of the more infuriating ironies of her art. But she often had work, and for that she was grateful. In one film she had performed a chilling scream, having discovered a corpse in an elevator. In another she played a whore lounging on a bordello couch in topaz lamplight. Once, in order to play a kleptomaniacal nanny caught stealing a lace handkerchief, she affected a cockney accent, using it for weeks, even to answer her phone. She was in a dozen crowd scenes. Off screen she had passing conversations with Bette Davis and Myrna Loy, not to mention coffee at the same commissary table as Fritz Lang.

By her own judgment, the camera had caught her in only one incandescent moment. It was in a movie called *The French Quarter*, shot, of course, in New Orleans. Lola played a sailor's night-on-the-town. She got drunk in an oyster bar, hoisted a chair above her head, and smashed a nickel-a-play jukebox. The box whirred and started up with "Why'd you have to leave me on a rainy day . . ." a wrenching refrain that Lola slurred. Staring inconsolably at the turning record, as if drawing from it the proper mood, she wobbled over to the sailor sitting at a round table, leaned her face close to his, and said, "When you ain't got a nickel, you've got to find a cheaper way to get sad." Sprawling across the table, she cupped her ear to catch the final notes of the song. The entire routine was ad-libbed. Had the female star come up with such a perfect invention, it would have been considered genius. But Lola was reprimanded by the director for having deviated from the script. Still, he kept the scene.

Back in 1943, only a month after they met on the Venice pier, Lola and Harry moved in together. They lived in a white, two-room cottage on Sepulveda Boulevard. It was in a horseshoe of cottages, with a cement fountain in the middle and two Art Deco swans whose bills lit up at night. But for an occasional meal at the Chili Château or Burger Palace, they'd most often dine on what Harry caught off the pier. Harry had on-and-off work at the studios and was a part-time instructor at an electronics school ten blocks from the apartment. The incident with Lorenzo hadn't exactly blacklisted him, but it hadn't helped much, either. Meanwhile, their closets filled with set designs.

At least once a week they'd stay on the pier all night, invigorated by the sea breezes, the plentiful rum, the lights of Los Angeles in the distance. They ignored the sign, as everyone did, that read PIER CLOSED 10 P.M.; now and then a policeman stopped to have a cup of coffee. Up and down the pier were lanterns, radios, lunch boxes. In the early hours, while their young children slept on cots, parents stood hunched over the railings, staring at the ocean, dozing off, waking up if a perch, snapper, or sea bass bent their poles. Sometimes a shark was pulled in and displayed on the pier, where it would thrash about as dogs snarled at it, keeping just out of reach. Some mornings, after waking to a thick, chill fog on her fold-up cot, Lola would take a bus directly to one of the studios and check the bulletin board for work. She'd smell like fish and salt air and would wash in the ladies' room sink.

They had ten years of this.

One early autumn morning in 1953, Lola looked out the window and saw Harry sitting on the cement rim of the pond. He had one foot propped up on a Deco swan and was reading a letter. Lola brought him out a cup of coffee and said, "Who's that from?"

"From my uncle Ted's lawyer," Harry said, handing Lola the letter.

Lola took the letter but didn't read it. "You sound worried," she said.

"Not exactly," Harry said. "It says that Teddy's died and left me his motel, back east in Vermont. It's called Unique Cabins."

"The place you spent blissful childhood days, I imagine," Lola said.

"Only one summer," Harry said. "I was ten. In fact, it's pretty much all I remember from being ten. There were these cabins, and different faces at breakfast every morning. My parents left me there for a couple of weeks. Uncle Teddy put me to work, raking, painting, that sort of thing. And there were chickens, all over the yard, like they'd escaped from the pen and didn't know where else to go. I was always tripping over chickens."

Lola read the letter slowly. "Harry," she said, "I've never

been to Vermont. I'm going to start packing." She sat down next to Harry, looking at him with a hopeful expression.

"I doubt there's even a repertory theater within a day's drive," Harry said. He sipped his coffee. Then he took the letter back from Lola and read it through again.

"Harry," Lola said, "sometimes something happens from outside your life, and it gives you a hint of what to try next. Just think about it. It doesn't have to mean we're failures here."

After a week of talking around the idea, rejecting it outright, arguing back through all the angles, Lola said over dinner, "Let's just sell a few things, pack up, and leave. I was ready the minute I read that letter."

"Well, I wasn't," Harry said. "But I am now."

There was a small going-away party for them out on the pier. Fried fish sandwiches and sponge cake for dessert. Harry and Lola didn't say where they were going, only that they wouldn't be fishing on the pier for at least a year. It was a brief, spirited party, after which everyone returned to the railings or their cots, tuning their radios according to the shifts the night air made in the reception. Harry and Lola spent the night there and in the morning had a yard sale.

They financed their move by escorting two enormous flatbed trucks, each hauling half a house, to a Cleveland suburb. They'd packed the Buick with clothes, the heads of the Deco swans sticking up from between piles of Hawaiian shirts. The law required that they place a flashing light atop the car and

attach a sign to the front and rear bumper that read OVER-
SIZED LOAD, referring to the flatbeds. Setting out from Hollywood one morning, they snailed along behind the two
trucks. The open end of each half of the house, cut through
the living room, was covered by sheet plastic that rippled and
snapped in the highway wind. Two weeks later they arrived
in Cleveland, sick of motels, of fed-up drivers yelling, "Get a
horse." The two house halves were unloaded and joined together, something Lola and Harry promised themselves they
would wait around to see.

They stopped for two days in Sandusky, where they stayed
in a hotel that had the largest porch they'd ever seen. It was
a luxury hotel, cheap in the off season. "Don't expect Unique
Cabins to have a porch like this," Harry said.

They continued on, relieved to be free of the moving
house. Three days later they pulled into a gas station in
Marshfield, a small town on Route 2 in upper Vermont. According to the letter, that was where Unique Cabins was located. It was the start of leaf season. Harry got out and leaned
against the car.

The station's owner, Bill Tekosky, an elderly man with a
stubble beard, walked over. "I ain't shaved yet," he said shyly.
"I live up there." He pointed to a small apartment over the
garage.

"Can you direct me to Unique Cabins?" Harry said.

"Closed down," Tekosky said. "Afraid old Ted's gone to
the motel in the sky." He didn't say it in a joking way.

"Well, I'm opening it up again," Harry said.

Tekosky looked at the Buick's plates. "California," he said. "Just east of Hawaii, right?"

"That's it," Harry said.

"So you came all the way from California to take over the bat mansion?" Tekosky said.

"That's about it," Harry said.

"Four miles down the road," Tekosky said, nodding west. "You passed it on your way here."

"Thanks much," Harry said. "The name's Harry Chappel. That's Lola in the car."

Lola gave a quick wave.

"You bet," Tekosky said.

They had Tekosky fill the gas tank, then drove slowly, taking in the scenery. A few farmhouses close to the road had pumpkins for sale, early Halloween decorations on their doors. "There it is," Lola said, pointing to a wooden sign with white lettering—UNIQUE CABINS—underneath a smaller sign, hanging by a chain, that read VACANCY. "Now that's honest," Lola said. "I like that."

Chickens scattered in the driveway as Harry guided the Buick in. "We're here. Let's take a stretch," he said.

They got out and meandered through a yard of overgrown grass and weeds. "Could use a manicure, right?" Lola said. There were eight peeling, dark green cabins situated in pairs. Each had a small porch with a stack of wood on it. A white house with an OFFICE sign and screened porch sat at the end of the driveway.

They drew together and held hands, realizing that this meant they were a little nervous about their new life. They stepped up onto the porch of the nearest cabin and were surprised to find the door open. Inside was a bedroom with oak paneling, a bathroom, and a small living room. Next to the bed was a night-stand with a radio and a gooseneck lamp on top.

"They're probably all pretty much the same, wouldn't you think, Lola?" Harry said.

"Yes, I would," Lola said. "I can't say exactly what, but there's something comforting about that."

A painting of rowers on a pond was on the wall above the bed. Harry imagined Uncle Ted walking into a store and saying, "I'll take eight of those." He laughed to himself. But envisioning Ted as he was twenty years ago suddenly saddened Harry. Glancing around the grounds, he saw that each cabin had a name printed in crude white letters on a slat of wood nailed above the door: Doreen, Edgar, Harry, Mitch, Bozzie, Lynn, Nellie, Jack. Harry recognized these as the names of his cousins, only two of whom—Edgar and Nellie—he'd ever met.

"You know," he said, "you're my entire family, Lola. I mean it, you are."

"These cabins put you in a mood," Lola said.

"I'm tired, just now," Harry said. "The driving, I guess."

Then Lola turned back the blanket and sheet of the bed. The linen was a little musty, but the autumn air was crisp. Lola unbuttoned the top button of Harry's shirt, and he did the rest. They made love and slept nearly until dusk. Waking almost together, Lola said, "Should we sleep here or in the main house?"

"Not here," Harry said. "We can't afford the prices."

In the last light of the day, they unloaded the car, aired out the main house, and set the Art Deco swans on the lawn where they could be seen from the road. At first, the chickens hurried over and lined up behind the swans, waiting for something to happen. But when Harry flicked the switches on the swan's necks, lighting up their bills, a rooster charged them, squalling loudly. After that the chickens kept their distance.

All of October they set up house. They painted the cabins barn red, and the house white again, but added black shutters. They repaired the cabins and house as much as they could afford to. During the remainder of the autumn, they had enough guests to keep them going. They didn't advertise; travelers just stopped in off the road. Lola cooked pancakes and scrambled eggs for the guests and brewed their coffee. Breakfast was served in what they called the Entertainment Center, a refurbished shed with a small kitchen area, two picnic tables, a radio, and a used TV with rabbit ears that Harry wrapped in aluminum foil for better reception. Lola and Harry were too busy to really assess how things were going, until one night Harry forced himself to examine the ledgers. "This is a real mess we've got here," he said to Lola. "Teddy was an idiot with numbers. He left some debts, and the repairs cost us more than I thought."

Lola knew that Harry's sudden realization could quickly gather into despair, even lead to rash decisions. Despite their years of poverty in California, they had never been in debt; Lola knew how the mere mention of debt shook Harry. But she couldn't bear the thought of giving up the cabins and having to move again. Besides, where would they go? So she said to Harry, weighing each word carefully, "Why not look at it this way? We don't have children. It's just the two of us. Let's give it another year. If the place gets on its feet, fine. If it goes under, we'll sell it or burn it or anything you decide. I just want to stay a while." Harry, persuaded more by Lola's weariness than her logic, realized he didn't want to move again, either.

That first year they closed down Unique Cabins for the season in early December. Snow would bring droves of skiers to Vermont, but the best hills for that were farther south and west; it wasn't worth keeping their place open. They brought in the electric heaters from each cabin and lined them up in the basement, covering them with tarp. Lola had become the bookkeeper; bills and invoices were neatly stacked on the dining room table. Once each week, she met with her canasta group, regaling everyone with lusty Hollywood tales, many of which she'd heard thirdhand. Otherwise Harry and Lola didn't go out much. Bowling on Friday nights. To a restaurant in Montpelier on Sundays. Lola liked seeing the gold dome of the capitol building there. Once in a while Harry ate a sandwich with Bill Tekosky or hung around the sawmill where he'd bought lumber to replace rotten boards at the cabins.

Working late into the winter nights, Harry kept up with his sketchbooks. They never left the kitchen where he worked, though. But obscurity isn't failure, he told himself; I had the talent, he thought, and still do. The world just won't know about it.

Lola never said a word about the sketchbooks.

By spring it was clear that they needed money, so Harry answered an ad and took a job managing the local drive-in. It was called the Moonlight and was about ten miles away, on the Barre-Montpelier road, about a mile outside of Montpelier. It had a wide gravel field of forty speakers, each on an iron pole. The drive-in was open every night except Monday, half price for children under twelve. The job meant Harry and Lola had to cancel their bowling night and go out to dinner on Monday night.

Harry hired two high school students to work the refreshment stand and a third to sell tickets from the entrance booth. He also hired George Morel, a retired policeman, to patrol for trouble. When regular customers complained that the old cop was a voyeur, that he sometimes peeked into their cars and looked a long time before shining his flashlight, Harry figured that it might be a strategy to get the man fired. He asked George Morel about it directly. "I'm not saying it's true or it isn't true," George Morel said, which took Harry aback slightly. "If it is true, though, can you blame me?" These were such oddly circuitous answers that Harry asked George Morel to stick close to the concession stand, which made him all but useless.

It was the 1950s, and a certain stifling morality prevailed, so Harry saw the Moonlight as an escape. Except for a few pranksters who occasionally careened through the gravel corridors between cars, honking horns, yelling obscenities, pulling their trousers down, or yanking speakers from the stands, Harry had little trouble. The customers, mostly teenagers, were too busy attending to what Harry called horizontal matters. He didn't care what went on in the cars. He slept in the projection booth, or read, or made small repairs around the refreshment stand. He brought popcorn home for Lola.

It was a transition time for movies; the golden age of film idols had ended, and the beach blanket craze was running amok. Harry spent long hours deciding how to order movies that would meet his own tastes yet still bring in money, and he did a good job of it. The owners kept him on. Truth was, people probably would have returned every weekend no matter what was showing. Still, Harry thought they should see something decent whenever they did decide to glance up at the screen. At the end of each movie, Harry always watched carefully to see if he recognized any of the technical crew's names on the credits.

That late March day in 1965, having thought back to *White Savage*, to leaving Los Angeles, and to their first year in Vermont, Harry had fallen asleep. Lola finished her pancake breakfast, walked into the living room, and nudged him awake. "Harry," she said, "wake up. We've got to start answering reservation letters."

Much of the summer was booked by May; after twelve years, though, their savings were small and Harry had had to stay on at the Moonlight.

"I was just dreaming," he said.

"What about?" Lola said. "Tell me, then let's get to the reservations."

"The birthday party we had for you on the pier," Harry said. "Remember?"

"Yes," Lola said, "the shark's-fin soup."

"The noodles," Harry said.

"Cupcakes with candles," Lola said. "It was sappy then, and still is."

Harry laughed. "Your birthday's coming around soon," he said. "About ten days, isn't it?"

"Don't remind me, Harry," Lola said.

"I didn't say a number, did I?" Harry said.

"Don't," Lola said.

"Well," Harry said, "whatever you want. I mean it. This year, whatever you want for your birthday is fine by me. Just let me know."

"Maybe a little tour west," Lola said. "Just *kidding*, Harry. Just kidding."

Harry said, "Here I'm trying to be . . ."

"Nice?" Lola said. "You were." She kissed the top of his head. "I'll think it over."

She went into the kitchen.

In a moment, Lola stood in the kitchen doorway and said, "Harry, I figured it out."

"What's that?" Harry said.

"My birthday," Lola said. "What I want for my birthday."

"Quick thinking," Harry said.

"I want to be on at the drive-in," Lola said.

"What's that?" Harry said, pretending not to have heard.

Enunciating each word clearly, Lola said, "I want to be on at the Moonlight."

"Make some sense, Lola," Harry said. "What are you talking about, exactly?"

"I don't think I can make it much clearer," Lola said.

"At the Moonlight?" Harry said.

"Correct," Lola said.

"In the winter," Harry said.

"Winter is when I was born," Lola said.

"In zero degrees," Harry said. "Maybe fifteen below, what with the wind chill."

"We'll show *White Savage*," Lola said. "That'll warm us up."

"Not that one," Harry said. "No possible way. How about *Forever Amber*?"

"*White Savage*," Lola said.

"Why torture us?" Harry said. "What about *The French Quarter*? That was a wonderful scene you did."

"It was wonderful, wasn't it?" Lola said. "But I want *White Savage* for my birthday."

"What about *Destination Tokyo*? Or *Cobra Woman*? You could team up with Jon Hall again. Montez, Sabu even. Lon Chaney. I almost forget about him! Chaney was in that picture, wasn't he?"

"You know he was," Lola said. "He was in *White Savage*, too. It'll be good to see the old boy again."

"Maybe twenty below," Harry said.

"Harry," Lola said, "you promised. Less than five minutes ago you said, 'Whatever you want.' "

"All *right*," Harry said. "Okay."

"Harry, you're pouting like a baby," Lola said, puffing out her lower lip. "You're still friends with Abe Katzenberg, aren't you? You hear from him once in a while, don't you?"

"He phones now and then," Harry said.

"Well, he's still with Universal, isn't he?" Lola said.

"Warner Brothers now," Harry said.

"You can write to him," Lola said. "Ask him for a print of *White Savage*. A loan. I'm sure he could arrange that, dig it out of the tombs. It's not exactly a movie people are clamoring for."

"We agree on that much," Harry said. "Okay, I'll write Abe."

"Maybe you should phone him," Lola said. "I want to see *White Savage* right on my birthday."

Harry trudged over to the phone and looked up Abe Katzenberg's number in his address book. "Three hours' time difference," he said. "Abe should just be waking up."

Harry dialed. After a few rings, he said, "Hello, Abe? It's me, Harry. Harry Chappel. Calling from Vermont. How's things? . . . Haven't spoke in a few months, so I thought I'd . . . Good. Great. Terrific. I'm so glad to hear it. Abe . . . listen, do you still have access to the archive? . . . Great. Because I'm calling out of the blue like this to ask a favor. . . . In ten days it's Lola's fiftieth. Yeah, no kidding. . . . She's fine. I'll tell her you asked. . . . What do you mean, what are we doing here in Vermont? Freezing our butts off, that's what. Same as last winter when we talked. It's fifteen degrees out, Abe. Maybe zero, what with the wind chill factor. Anyway, listen, Abe. I'd like a print of that movie *White Savage*. . . . Yeah, that's the one. Believe me, Abe, I feel the same way you do about it. Remember who you're talking to here. . . . Yeah, I know. But it's the one Lola wants. No, we're getting along fine. Can you arrange it? . . . In a week? Terrific. Wonderful, Abe. Abe, I can't thank you enough. Kiss Beth and the kids for us, will you? You got the address? . . . Right, yeah. . . . Okay, I'll tell her. So long, Abe."

Harry put down the receiver.

"Thank you, Harry," Lola said. "This means something to me."

Nine days later, *White Savage* arrived at the Marshfield Post Office in a cardboard box marked FRAGILE. Back at home, Harry placed the round metal canister on the kitchen table and read out loud the note Abe Katzenberg had taped to the film's spool. "Hope seeing this film doesn't break up a happy twosome! Don't freeze out there. And don't be such strangers. Love, Beth and Abe."

"That's sweet," Lola said.

Harry stared at the film. "Down the toilet," he muttered. He placed the canister in a cupboard and kept to the living room the rest of the day.

Harry spent much of Lola's birthday at the Moonlight, clearing the high drifts of snow from the entrance with his snow-blowing machine. Wearing his Monty Clift shirt, two sweaters, a goosedown coat, thick corduroy trousers, galoshes, earmuffs, and a wool hat with earflaps, he unlocked the gate, swung it open, then cleared a path to the ticket booth. From there, snow fanning out from the machine in blurred sweeps, he made his way to the refreshment stand, making sure the path was wide enough for his truck. After opening the stand, he went back to the pickup truck he'd bought a year before, drove past the ticket booth, and parked near the stand. Holding the print of *White Savage*, he stomped his feet on the door stoop, went inside, and turned on the heat. Dust drifted out of the floor vents. He sat down by a vent and groaned,

"Twelve years in this icebox." The stand felt like a small-town bus depot, with the candy and soda ads as garish as travel posters. Out the wide front window, the screen loomed like a wall of ice. A few crows perched on top of it. There was snow halfway up each speaker pole, and the speakers themselves were capped with hard snow as well.

After warming up a little, Harry went back outside and took up the blowing machine again. He cut a wide swath through the snow to a speaker directly in front of the stand. He then worked the machine until it had cleared away a space large enough for his truck. After stopping to rest, he took out his pocketknife and chipped the snow crust from the speaker they would use that night. Returning to the stand, he climbed the short flight of stairs to the projection booth and put *White Savage* on the reel. He was half tempted to run it through once, to see if the crows would flee the screen. Instead, he got on the phone to Lola. "It's all set," he said. "I'll be home in a little while." He flicked on the lights of the refreshment stand and those lining the driveway. He walked out and chipped away snow from the driveway lights; they all worked fine. Then he drove home.

Harry placed his galoshes over the floor heat vent by the back door, took off his coat and hat and one of his sweaters, and sat down at the table. Lola had made steak, potatoes au gratin, and a salad. She lit candles, poured them each a glass of red wine, and lifted her glass. "Why should I make the toast?" she said.

"It's maybe twenty below, all things considered," Harry said. "Happy birthday, Lola."

They tapped glasses and said little during dinner. They put on their coats, galoshes, and hats; and Harry went out to warm up the truck. Then Lola came out. It took about half an hour to get to the Moonlight because it was snowing lightly and the roads had iced up, so Harry drove slowly. At the Moonlight, he all but coasted over sheet ice past the ticket booth.

He maneuvered the truck into place by the speaker; new snow had already covered the places he'd cleared earlier.

"Keep the engine running," Harry said. "We'll need the heat. Just make sure to crack the window open a little, okay?"

"I'll put the speaker in place," Lola said. "All the snow you took care of!"

"Don't mention it," Harry said.

He got out and walked to the refreshment stand, opened the door, and went upstairs. He sat on the swivel chair and started up the projector. It was dark outside now, with hazy light filtering through the gray-blanketed clouds. Then the screen was full of color. As the opening credits appeared, there was an aerial view of a tropical island: coral reefs, blue-green water. Drums throbbed, receding whenever racing violins introduced a star's name: Jon Hall, Maria Montez, Lon Chaney, and *presenting* Sabu.

"Flush it down," Harry groaned.

He stayed in the booth until, on screen, Lola and Maria

Montez were dragged screaming from the village. He walked back to the truck, got in, and snuggled up to Lola in an exaggerated way.

"Stop it, Harry," Lola said. "And I mean it." Harry moved as far from Lola as possible, but watched her as she watched the movie. Her face showed nostalgia and vulnerability, and Harry turned back to the screen.

"There you are again!" Harry said, advancing the obvious as enthusiasm.

On screen, Lola was thrashing about, strapped by her wrists, shouting, "Help! Help!" Monkeys clicked and chirred down at her. A vermilion parrot nodded and squawked.

"What a goddam menagerie," Harry said.

"Shhhhh!" Lola said, turning up the volume.

A thick, mottled snake flickered its tongue and unraveled down the length of a viny branch.

"Help!" Lola screamed, appealing to the jungle at large. "For God's sake, somebody help me!"

"It was a godless place," Harry said. "If they'd used *my* jungle, God would've been present, but you still would've died."

Lola turned to him and narrowed her eyes.

Forty minutes passed with Harry fidgeting and Lola raptly attentive to the screen.

"Oh, well," Lola sighed. She lit a cigarette.

Harry looked up at the screen. Poor Lola was now a skeleton.

"Do you still have that blouse?" Harry asked, truly curious, though Lola, silent, took it as patronizing.

"You want to stay for the rest?" Harry said.

"Yes, Harry, I do," Lola said. "I do want to stay. That's my birthday present up there, in case you forgot."

"Sorry," Harry said, holding up his hands as if under arrest. "I only meant, if it's upsetting you . . ."

"That's not what you meant," Lola said.

After a few minutes, she said dreamily, "I want to stay until the end. Then I'd like you to go back and turn off the projector so the screen has just its own light again. As a kid I used to love lying in bed in the dark. It always amazed me that there was always some light in the room, no matter how dark it was outside. Even with my eyes closed. Such a simple thing."

Out on the road a few cars slowed down, their drivers and passengers surprised to see a movie flickering through falling snow. But no one turned into the driveway.

Lola said, "That scene when the camera is directly on me, just before the cannibals arrive. Just by campfire light that way, with everything about my face and character calm and brave and just right. When I was a girl, that's who I wanted to be."